ALIETTE DE BODARD

OF DRAGONS, FEASTS
AND MURDERS

ALSO BY ALIETTE DE BODARD

OBSIDIAN AND BLOOD
Servant of the Underworld*
Harbinger of the Storm*
Master of the House of Darts*

DOMINION OF THE FALLEN
The House of Shattered Wings
The House of Binding Thorns
The House of Sundering Flames†

DRAGONS AND BLADES
Of Dragons, Feasts and Murders*
Of Charms, Ghosts and Grievances*

XUYA UNIVERSE
On a Red Station, Drifting
The Citadel of Weeping Pearls*
The Tea Master and the Detective^
Of Wars, and Memories, and Starlight

SHORT FICTION AND NOVELLAS
In the Vanishers' Palace*
Of Books, and Earth, and Courtship

* available as a JABberwocky edition worldwide
† available as a JABberwocky edition in North America
^ available as a JABberwocky edition outside of North America

OF DRAGONS, FEASTS AND MURDERS

A DRAGONS AND BLADES STORY

ALIETTE DE BODARD

JABberwocky Literary Agency, Inc.

Of Dragons, Feasts and Murders
by Aliette de Bodard

This paperback edition published in 2021. Originally published in 2020 by JABberwocky Literary Agency, Inc., in association with the Zeno Agency LTD.

http://www.awfulagent.com/ebooks

ISBN 978-1-625675-83-5

"Tet is a feast that's a bit like Christmas." Thuan realized his mistake as soon as he'd spoken. He'd meant to compare Lunar New Year to something familiar, something every Parisian would respect, but he'd underestimated how little his husband cared about social norms. Or religion: for all that he was a Fallen angel, Asmodeus had always been summarily uninterested in anything so inconsequential—and unattainable—as redemption.

Asmodeus—sitting on the four-poster bed in the quarters they'd been assigned in the imperial citadel of the dragon kingdom—raised an eyebrow. "What makes you think House Hawthorn celebrates Christmas?"

"Good food and the company of your loved ones?" Thuan was sitting in one of the carved mahogany chairs, the straight-backed and uncomfortable ones of his childhood. He hadn't missed these at all.

"The House's version of Christmas involved rather less love, and more bodies dangling in trees."

"And your version?"

An expansive shrug that Thuan knew all too well.

"You don't celebrate, do you."

Asmodeus's face was an eloquent statement in and of itself. He sat on the bed, looking distant and sarcastic, an act which Thuan knew masked profound worry. "I'm here with you. I've, ah, *volunteered* for more than my fill of celebration." An accent on the word that suggested something wholly unpleasant. He reached out, smoothing the lapels of his swallowtail jacket almost absent-mindedly. His grey-green gaze, behind his square horn-rimmed glasses, was matter-of-fact, unemotional, but that didn't mean a lot, as he was supremely adept at disguising his own emotions. "You should be happy." It sounded like nothing so much as a threat.

Trouble was, Thuan wasn't really sure he was.

Tet was a time for celebration: a changing of the lunar year, a chance to start anew without debts, to turn the course of fate. A time to go home to celebrate with family, and it had been an eternity since Thuan had gone home to the underwater kingdom of the Seine, an eternity since he'd seen Second Aunt—the Empress who ruled over the *rông*, the shape-shifting Annamite dragons such as Thuan.

And what better way to go home than to bring one's own husband, to show him the imperial citadel bedecked with trees and garlands of algae and yellow flowers and share with him the delights of banquets?

The first problem was, unsurprisingly, that Asmodeus was on edge: he didn't like being away from home, in a place where he had no means of pressure on anyone. Home was House Hawthorn, which he and Thuan co-ruled: a maze of grandiose buildings, outhouses and gardens in the midst of a ruined and devastated Paris—a fortress both physical and magical that was meant to safeguard all their dependents, from Fallen angels to mortals and dragons, from magicians and alchemists to gardeners and bodyguards. Hawthorn had recently been devastated by an attack from another House, and Thuan and Asmodeus were currently struggling to rebuild it while keeping everyone secure.

The second, and most important problem was that Thuan's memories of the imperial citadel had been utterly accurate, and this time he didn't have the excuse of being trapped in it: he'd walked into it out of his own free will. The court was best described as a seething mass of hornets, and that was the understatement of the millennium. If Asmodeus was on edge, Thuan was much worse—he'd never felt so exposed, his foreigner husband only the lowest item on a long list of liabilities that started with his incapacity to know how his words would be misinterpreted and by which faction.

"I'm sure my aunt is happy," he said. She'd recently

Aliette de Bodard

declared herself Empress rather than Princess, finally acknowledging what everyone had known for decades: that she was the ruling power of the dragon kingdom and not merely an accidental heir as her father's eldest living child.

"Good," Asmodeus said. He turned to the bedside table—where he'd managed to store an impressive array of enchanted knives—and picked up his book. "That makes at least one of us. Now if you'll excuse me, I was rather looking forward to how our rather anemic hero found the secret passage in the attic."

Obviously he was too observant to fail to notice Thuan's deflection.

Thuan sighed, and went looking for clothes. Their quarters were a wide, airy suite in one of the palaces of the citadel reserved for dignitaries: a single room with cracked tiled floors, and pillars leading up to wooden rafters carved with the serpentine shape of dragons and various prosperity signs. The air was charged with brine, the light heavy, causing everything to undulate slightly, as if they'd been back on land staring through a heatwave. Except, of course, that they were underwater, in that peculiar bubble of the kingdom where they could breathe normally, but where coral and algae grew in gardens, and where little crabs and salamanders scuttled between the cracks of the floor.

A lacquered screen separated the room in two parts, a bedroom with a massive four-poster bed on which Asmodeus was currently lounging with his book, and a

4

reception room with a table and two wooden high-backed benches, the table polished teak wood with straight legs, something straight out of the traditionalist fashion. They'd put their clothes in the reception room, in the four stacked chests of clothes, each marked with the name of a season—never mind that they hadn't brought enough with them to fill more than a fraction of the chests.

The citadel, like the rest of the dragon kingdom and the rest of Paris, had been hard-hit by the war, and everything might have looked grandiose and polished from a distance, but the rot was everywhere: under Thuan's feet, the floor was full of minute cracks; the table was scored with various gouges; and the wooden ceiling had been hastily glued back together, and was already showing signs of algae and mould.

They had a banquet at the bi-hour of the rooster, and he'd need to make sure he picked the right clothes: Asmodeus could probably get away with any of the swallowtail suits he'd brought, the black brocade jackets with ever-different patterns that the officials and courtiers would find exciting or dismiss as insufficiently adhering to the rules. The rest of their delegation could wear House Hawthorn uniform and play the role of retainers. Thuan, unfortunately, would have to remember where the married-off son of the third sister of the empress fitted into the palace hierarchy. Was he entitled to a red dress with yellow dragons; and what about the hairpins and the brooches?

The door opened. Thuan braced himself for an official,

but there was no sound—except that, after a while, it swung back; and when he looked up, Asmodeus was gone.

What—?

His mind immediately ran to the worst-case scenarios—kidnapping, murder, which just showed how on edge he was. This was all ridiculous. He got up in one fluid gesture, half-shifting into his dragon shape—a huge and serpentine water spirit with stubby legs, his antlers nudging the carvings of the ceiling. He pushed the door open with an enormous snout—just in time to see Asmodeus vanish around the corner of the courtyard just outside their room, taking a pillared corridor leading to another building complex.

Typical.

Thuan stifled a curse, and flew after him, mentally rehearsing how he'd convince Asmodeus not to go wandering into strange places without at least warning him—he could already imagine the argument they'd have, Asmodeus insisting he didn't need to be coddled (which was totally true, but Thuan was also thinking of these unfortunate people who'd stand in his path, and the diplomatic incidents that could ensue).

Thuan slid into the corridor, between the red-lacquered pillars: it snaked between the other rooms, and finally opened onto another paved courtyard with a central statue of three emperors, their cracked stone features eaten by algae.

The courtyard was full of people: variegated officials in jade five-panel tunics with rank patches and winged hats, courtiers with the same tunics but without the hats, and people of the lowest ranks.

Where—

But he didn't really need to look far to find Asmodeus, because his husband was kneeling by the side of a corpse.

For a moment Thuan stood frozen in horrified fascination, mentally rehearsing all the excuses he could summon, all the diplomatic precedents of extraterritorial jurisdiction in the archives of the court—that time Ambassador Ghislaine had been lured out of the citadel, no, that wouldn't do, because she'd left of her own free will—something else then, before the arrival of Fallen, maybe the Minister of Rites being slapped by an envoy of the Bièvre? He distantly noticed that the corpse was lying at the foot of a short flight of stairs leading into a palace. It was that of an official of uncertain gender, their topknot pinned by silver hairpins—not a high-ranking one, then, but someone who did have a rank. He couldn't see wounds, but the embroidered tunic was soaked with blood, a smell that covered the usual background one of incense, algae and mildew that pervaded the ruined citadel. The contents of their sleeves had spilled on the floor: strings of cash, folded papers, and their personal seal, so deeply soaked with blood the jade had turned dark.

And then he noticed that Asmodeus's face was creased in fascination, and that the Fallen magic trembling over the body was a spell of reconstitution—something to tell him how the person had died. So he hadn't killed them.

Good.

An irate-looking third-rank official pushed their way through the crowd and said, "Excuse me! This isn't business for foreigners."

Asmodeus barely looked up. "You all seemed to be talking a lot and not doing much. The smell of blood was so overwhelming I could feel it from my quarters."

Which explained why he'd left the room, though Thuan doubted very much it had been with the intention of complaining about it, but rather with an aroused curiosity on a possible nearby source of entertainment.

A tug, on the spines of his serpentine body. He whipped round, his body curling into a full circle, his antlers ready to butt into the invader—but it was merely his cousin Hong Chi. "A word," she said. She was wearing full court dress: a brocade red robe with phoenixes in flight in the midst of thickets of good-luck flowers, and her topknot was impeccably held by golden hairpins, her face lightly painted over with ceruse and her lips the red of carmine.

Thuan threw a glance at the scene, where the official had been joined by two others, brandishing rites and propriety. A very familiar expression of growing annoyance was freezing Asmodeus's face.

"Oh, he'll be fine," Hong Chi said, a tad impatiently. "He'll eat them for breakfast and you know it."

"Which he's kind of not supposed to do," Thuan said,

but he still followed her back into the courtyard in front of their quarters. It was a smaller affair: a simple paved space with a few coral reefs in ornamental shapes, a breathing space between nested palaces that were so close to each other they'd become a single building.

"What's going on?"

Hong Chi grimaced. "Do you know Kim Diep?"

"You *know* I haven't been at court for two years," Thuan said. "Is that the corpse's name?"

"She's a concubine of the third rank. She administrates the gardens of Peaceful Contemplation."

So not the corpse, then. "I'm not too sure—"

"She killed them. The corpse," Hong Chi said.

"So let me get this straight. You don't know who the corpse is, but you know who killed them?"

An annoyed snort from Hong Chi. She wasn't wearing her full dragon shape: the antlers were visible above her topknot, faintly translucent. A patch of rot in the hollow of her collarbones had been expertly disguised with ceruse. "You do know I'm in charge of the secret police these days."

Thuan weighed the cost of admitting his ignorance, and decided he didn't care. Hong Chi had a host of other names and titles now, but to Thuan she'd always remain the little dragon girl who'd raced him to the top of the Bell and Drum Towers in the city. "I'm out of touch."

"Good," Hong Chi said. "Because being in touch is dangerous business."

"You're not making sense."

An exhaled breath from Hong Chi—a ghostly snout superimposing itself on the redness of her lips. "It's been bad years, as you well know. Crops dying in the fields, the angel essence epidemic, weird animals showing up in the imperial gardens that no one can identify or catch…"

Thuan was starting to see where this was going, and he didn't like it. "Instability," he said, because he didn't want to say the other words aloud.

Hong Chi had never been one for mincing words. "There are whispers that the dynasty has lost the Mandate of Heaven."

Which was bad, because that was usually a prelude to rebellion. "Surely Second Aunt is trying to turn things around."

A snort. "Of course. Fixing dikes and famine is a long-term process. And getting rid of corrupt officials is a long and arduous process: if she throws them all out at once, she's going to lose the supporters of her throne. At least the angel essence epidemic has stopped—" she eyed Thuan, daring him to contradict her.

Thuan met her gaze levelly. House Hawthorn had been involved in that particular drug traffic, but that had been prior to his accession to power—and without Asmodeus's knowledge. They and the other Houses were now united into stopping the flow of essence into the dragon kingdom. "That shouldn't be a problem anymore, no." But he could see her point: all of this was going to require time to fix, and it increasingly looked like they were running out of it. "I still don't see where Kim Diep fits in."

"Kim Diep is at the forefront of people agitating against the Empress," Hong Chi said. "She's unhappy, bearing a lot of grudges, and no one would be happier than her to see the entire thing coming down."

It still didn't make sense. "So you have evidence, and you haven't arrested her yet?"

"I have evidence of a loose tongue," Hong Chi said. "That isn't a crime, not these days." A mirthless laugh. "We're *modern* now."

"But you're sure the murderer is her," Thuan said.

"Because of this. I took it from the body before people got a good look at it." Hong Chi's hand dived into her sleeve, and came up with what looked like cash—but on closer inspection turned out to be a single copper coin engraved with a stylised word surrounded by the eight trigrams.

Battle.

Thuan flipped it over, and saw letters bunched together so tightly they weren't recognisable anymore.

"Ten thousand victories, a single harmony," Hong Chi said, somberly. "The Harmony of Heaven. They're a secret society with too many ambitious officials."

"Ah." And one of them, doubtless, who wanted to be crowned empress or emperor of a new dynasty.

"I know what you're going to say. Membership of a secret society *is* a crime, but I don't have proof of Kim Diep being a member," Hong Chi said. "I have very suggestive evidence they want to move against Second Aunt on or shortly after Tet, and equally suggestive things that they have an agent in the citadel in an important position. And Kim Diep is very likely that agent. But nothing amounting to enough evidence to make an arrest. Or, more importantly, to thwart them."

"All right," Thuan said, trying to sound casual and not altogether succeeding, because changes of dynasty meant nothing good for the current one. "What do you want from me?"

Hong Chi smiled. "As you said—you're out of touch. And you're both visitors to the court."

"Which is my home," Thuan said, more sharply than he'd meant.

Hong Chi held out a hand, squeezing on his antlers. "It is. I'm sorry, I didn't mean to imply that way. It's just you're not part of any faction, or likely to be used by one, and your husband is…" She had that familiar face of people trying to describe Asmodeus in positive terms.

"A loose cannon," Thuan said. He smiled. "I'm in love with him, not blind."

"No one will mind if you jostle the bounds of propriety. Or if you get involved in affairs that aren't your business."

Whereas she, even as head of the secret police, would be curtailed in what she could and could not do—and in what enemies she could afford to make, for the sake of her own survival. A dance Thuan was all too familiar with. "You want me to find out why the corpse died, what Kim Diep is up to, and possibly what the society is up to if these turn out to be two different things. I didn't come here for that," he said. In fact, he'd come here in the hopes he could finally enjoy the citadel, instead of having to barricade himself in the library to avoid court intrigues.

"I know." Hong Chi's face was grave. "It's a big favour to ask."

She was expecting him to say no, in fact—a thought belatedly occurring to him when he saw the way she held herself, braced for rejection the same way she'd always been when they were children and she'd come up with yet another adventurous idea. Thuan thought of Second Aunt, of his cousins; of the citadel and all it contained set afire. "But fine. I'll see what I can do."

"An investigation? Into matters of disloyalty? With powers to ignore the constraints of the law?" Asmodeus looked like a child who'd just been handed a red envelope full of unexpected money. "I stand corrected. This might be rather less boring a stay than I'd thought."

Thuan had—with difficulty—managed to separate him from the corpse and three rather chastened officials, and they were now back in their quarters, waiting to hear from Thuan's request for an audience with Kim Diep. Asmodeus was sitting on the bed, sipping from a tea cup, and Thuan was trying not to stress-eat any of the candied fruit in the bowls on the table.

"You examined the corpse," he said.

"Yes," Asmodeus said. "I'm surprised you didn't ask to."

Thuan sighed. He should have, but since Hong Chi wasn't going to officially help him—at least not in front of officials—it would have taken a great deal of arguing with the court, something the prospect of which had been exhausting. "I don't have authority," he said, curtly. "Can you tell me about it?"

"Middle-aged woman—a crab, I think? She was a supervisor in the imperial kitchens. Her name was Ai Linh, according to one of these really annoying officials." Asmodeus relaxed against the bedpost.

"Ai Linh," At least Asmodeus's Viet had improved in leaps and strides, and he could manage to get through basic conversation these days. "How did she die?"

"In excruciating pain."

"Is that really relevant?" Thuan asked, more sharply than he'd meant.

"It rather depends if that was the main point, or a side-effect to death."

"Remind me never to bring you over for Tet ever again."

A silence. Thuan found Asmodeus in front of him, a finger resting on his lips—and then Asmodeus's mouth on his, kissing him long and deep until he shivered—and Asmodeus's hands, gently pressing on his shoulders until knots he hadn't been aware of came loose. "Asmodeus," he said, when he finally came up for air.

Asmodeus released him, but didn't move away from

him—his perfume of bergamot and orange blossom trembled in the air between them. "Poor sweet dragon prince. I'm finding this rather exciting, but you're angry and terrified, aren't you?" It was phrased like a question, but it wasn't really one.

Thuan could hardly deny the obvious. "Mmm. I'm not sure I want to talk about it."

Asmodeus's hand tipped his chin up, to look into his eyes. "You do."

"Confession being good for the soul?"

A short laugh. "You do because you need to convince me why we have to do this at all. Right now I'm feeling more inclined to have a word with that cousin of yours and make her change her mind about roping you in to do her dirty work."

That got his attention. "You can't touch her." *That* would be a diplomatic mess of epic proportions.

"I don't need to. I can be very... persuasive."

And he probably could, at that: he'd not risen to become head of House Hawthorn through being unsubtle. Thuan exhaled. "I've not really talked about my life before, in the imperial court."

"Hmm." Asmodeus hadn't moved. He cocked his head as if assessing Thuan, and finally said, "You were a bookish prince who became my betrothed when the field became short of candidates."

"Yes," Thuan said. A pause, but this was his husband, and if he couldn't say it to Asmodeus, then to whom? "I was the son of a minor sister of the imperial family. No one really expected me to be at court until my grandfather died and the power passed to my eldest aunt, and she decided every close kin member had to move there."

"Ah." A pause: still that odd expression on Asmodeus's face, inquisitive but aware he was getting close to weakness. "You were unused to it."

"I hated every minute of it. The different factions, all my cousins intriguing to be named crown princess, the courtiers, the concubines and the officials, and a never-ending flood of who was allied to whom, the memorials to be read and double-read to be sure I hadn't missed any meaning and knowing my allowance and position depended on that…" He was sitting on the bed and he wasn't sure how he'd got there anymore, and there was that tight feeling in his belly, the room being too small and constricted until he thought he was going to choke. He tried to laugh, found only searing emptiness in his mouth. "Bookish. I liked the library. The head archivist let me hide at the back of the shelves, and at least books by dead people have a pretty straightforward agenda."

He stopped, then. Asmodeus was standing next to him—looming over him, his broad frame encased in his embroidered jacket. He laid a hand on Thuan's shoulder, squeezed, lightly. "Oh, dragon prince. You're doing a terrible job of convincing me we're staying here at all."

Thuan snorted. "You think Hawthorn is better? It's got exactly the same intrigues."

A raised eyebrow. "It does. But you rule Hawthorn."

Some comfort. But of course it would be, to Asmodeus.

In his world, problems were solved by power, or pressure, or violence, or better yet, all three concurrently. "It wasn't all bad. I love my cousins. Well, some of them. Hong Chi and I used to share durian cakes in secluded courtyards, and she'd always bring me the memorials that mattered— and she did it because she loved me. And Second Aunt meant well. Politics would have found me even in my backwater countryside, and it'd have eaten me alive if I hadn't been prepared."

"You mean she chose to break you herself rather than watch you be broken."

"I'm not broken!"

"No," Asmodeus said. He sounded... angry? Thuan wasn't sure he found that reassuring at all, because the target was very clearly Second Aunt. "I meant she tried very hard and failed." A pause, then. "You love her." He sounded surprised. Or disapproving. Or both.

"She's my aunt," Thuan said. And, more simply, "She made me what I am."

A snort. "Rather. You're failing spectacularly to convince me I should expend effort trying to save the woman's throne."

Thuan sighed. Explaining duty or family wasn't going to terribly impress Asmodeus, but he had to try. "A change of dynasty usually means every descendant of the previous one comes to a messy end. That's all my remaining family in the dragon kingdom, even the ones who're not at court." He didn't wait to see his husband's face. "I know. I'm no longer part of the imperial family because I married out, and you think we'd be fine even in the middle of an upheaval, but I'd be really upset if those deaths happened."

"Hmm." Asmodeus didn't look really convinced.

Thuan squeezed Asmodeus's hand, trying very hard to hide the fact that something felt terribly loose in his chest. At least his parents were in House Hawthorn now. They were also coming into the dragon kingdom for Tet, but much closer to the New Year's Eve banquet: they'd never liked the court and Thuan had thought to spare them a long stay, but it turned out they'd be spared in other ways too. "Think of it as the meetings of the Court of House in Hawthorn. Boring and painful but necessary for longer term goals."

Asmodeus's face didn't move. "Fine," he said. "But if any point you look to be in too much distress, I'm marching you out of the kingdom and back home." A smile that was as thin as a knife wound. "And I'll take great pleasure in cutting down anyone who tries to tell me otherwise."

"All right." Thuan didn't feel like he had enough energy to argue. "Can we talk about Ai Linh now?"

A shrug. "Yes."

"You said she died in pain. But specifically of what?"

"Enspelled weapon," Asmodeus said. "But the murderer was either very sloppy or needed information from her, because I counted fifteen different wounds." He paused, considering for a while. "The first ones were deliberate, but after these she'd have slipped into shock quite fast."

"She's a crab," Thuan said. "Wasn't it what you said? Rông or other supernatural sea spirits heal fast. I don't think she'd have gone into shock."

"She would."

"You sound very certain."

"Yes," Asmodeus said. "And before you malign me, that's not because I experimented on your dragons in Hawthorn. It's just because one of them had an accident with an enspelled weapon in the Court of Persuasion when I was there. And really, I thought you'd know that kind of thing."

"I don't have personal experience," Thuan said, mildly.

"I figured you wouldn't. But it's your weaknesses we're talking about."

"That I'd appreciate being informed of," Thuan said, drily. He didn't push it further, because he knew Asmodeus did sarcasm as easily as he breathed—but he wasn't about to let him get away with just anything.

"Consider yourself informed now." Asmodeus didn't miss a beat. "Anyway, the next wounds are more frenzied." A pause. "I take it back, I don't think it's sloppiness. The murderer was running out of time."

"Mmm," Thuan said. "That's not terribly useful to find out why the society singled her out. Do you think they got what they wanted?"

"I don't think so." Asmodeus foraged inside his jacket pocket, and threw something on the table. It was an empty pouch of purple silk.

"She found it. What are we talking about here?"

"It was in her... carapace?" Asmodeus sounded uncertain. "The armoured bit on her chest and belly. I noticed it was a bit loose when I examined her, though there was a spell to make it seem normal unless one was paying special attention."

"You broke a *khi*-water spell with Fallen magic?" Thuan didn't know whether to feel impressed or horrified. Or both. Fallen had had little experience with *khi*-elements, the native magic of the Annamites: Fallen could practise it like everyone else, but most found it beneath them, or considered it quaint and weak. As a result, most of them were defenseless against the spells of the dragon kingdom. Asmodeus had never shown any interest in the magic, or so Thuan assumed.

"You dragged me into the dragon kingdom. Was I supposed to show up there defenseless?"

Of course not. "I'd say I'd want to be informed but you already knew that."

"Spoilsport."

Thuan bit back the obvious answer, and bent over the pouch. There was a single, faded character on it he didn't recognise—he couldn't even tell if it was meant to be Chinese or southern characters. Traces of a pale opalescent powder clung to the inside, and a faint glow of *khi*-water lay over them, a shimmering haze that was oddly fascinating.

Asmodeus's hand grabbed his and pulled it away—he hadn't even seen Asmodeus move. He held Thuan's hand in a grip of iron and refused to let go. "Ouch. Asmodeus—"

"Don't touch it," Asmodeus said. "She quite blithely hid it on herself, but you don't even know what it is."

"Poison? Surely—"

"Surely a few grains isn't enough to be deadly?" Asmodeus's face said, quite clearly, that Thuan was being breathtakingly naive for believing that.

"You don't do poisons."

"As a weapon, no. As something I need to defend against, I can assure you I studied extensively."

"Fine. So our murderer wanted a pouch of mysterious powder from someone who worked in the kitchens." The immediate deduction wasn't hard. "The banquet. The New Year's Eve one."

"Ah, yes. If someone from the close imperial family dies—if all of them die—that'd certainly make quite an impression."

Thuan shook his head. "Doesn't even need to be that bad. You're jumping to the catastrophe scenarios—" he tried, and failed, to remove the vivid images of dragons writhing in agony on tiled floors—"but things are already really bad in the kingdom. All the society need to do is imply bad fortune."

"Like what?"

"I don't know! Like making all the banh tet be rotted inside, or the tray of five abundance fruit fall to dust on the ancestral altar. It doesn't need to be *big*, it just needs to be significant."

"Ah. Superstition."

Thuan stared at him, and bit back on the first, angry

response. "No, appearances. That time you were at House Silverspires for Lady Selene's birthday and the gifts caught fire? That was a statement that didn't require deaths. It said, very clearly, that she didn't have the means to protect her own belongings. Same thing here. The Mandate of Heaven is about a dynasty's capacity to take care of its own people and possessions, and the right to rule it confers them as a result. We're not quaint, unenlightened inferiors."

A silence. Then Asmodeus said, stiffly, "I shouldn't have said that."

Thuan breathed out. "It's ok," he said, finally, though he still felt winded.

A look that could have split stone. "Don't you even dare apologise, dragon prince."

Thuan swallowed the words he'd been meaning to say. "Fine," he said, finally. "Now what?"

Thuan stood on top of the steps of the Flower Peace residence in the six chambers, waiting for a eunuch to come and retrieve him. He'd sent a request for an audience with Kim Diep earlier: he had signed it with his personal seal, which was all he had left. Once, he'd had another one as well, an official one that went with his title—just as the Empress herself had a host of seals she used for official purposes, and a personal one for her private correspondence. He'd had to surrender that when he'd married Asmodeus, obviously—he'd never missed it, but now that he was back in the citadel he had complex feelings about what he'd left behind.

Fortunately, Kim Diep had not seemed to care about his lack of titles, and had sent back a swift agreement to an audience.

It had been touch and go, for a while, on whether Asmodeus would let him out of the room at all—he was possessive normally, and being on edge just made it worse. Thuan had had to argue quite strenuously on how utterly weak he'd look if he showed up for interviewing a concubine with his husband darkly hovering like an overbrooding, over-aggressive bodyguard. Finally, he'd dispatched Asmodeus to investigate the mysterious powder, and to haunt the kitchens asking about Ai Linh.

The chambers were really a long, narrow palace building, its entrance lined with pillars and bathed in the dappled light of the underwater kingdom. The courtyard around them was huge: a clear separation between the six chambers, a space reserved for concubines and that had traditionally been difficult to access for anyone not of imperial blood or not a eunuch, and the rest of the citadel.

A trio of smiling youths passed him by—two men and a woman, all wearing the concubines' round flower and mango-bird insignia and giggling as they went towards the coral gardens—the woman was half in dragon shape, antlers framing her topknot, and scales on her cheeks, while both the men looked to be fish, with the same scales on their cheek but less sharply defined fingers and bulging eyes on either side of an almost inexistent nose.

Finally, a silent eunuch came, and led him to the east side of the stairs, to a small room entirely enclosed by a longevity lattice. Someone was waiting for him there, kneeling on cushions and blowing iridescent bubbles through a mother-of-pearl pipe. "Child," Kim Diep said, smiling and showing entirely too many pointed teeth in her mouth. An underwater animal, but the predator kind: an orca, with two white-eye spots just above her small, round eyes, and dark skin that shone in the lantern light. She was younger than him but married to his aunt, and that was the relationship that counted.

"Elder aunt," Thuan said, bowing. The way she smiled, he wasn't sure if he should have used a more appropriate title.

She had a youth-in-waiting with her, unobtrusively kneeling near the teapot, head bowed. The eunuch took his place near the door, to make sure that nothing untoward happened during the interview. Thuan wasn't surprised. Concubines might have more responsibilities than a symbol of sexual achievement those days, but propriety was still respected—and there was no way his aunt would tolerate a concubine's affair.

Not that he intended to commit incest with someone married to his aunt—it'd have been ludicrous, disgusting and utterly against benevolence and propriety.

The youth poured some tea, green and delicate and

utterly unlike the tea Asmodeus made at home—he'd never gotten the hang of water temperature or shorter brewing time, and everything ended up tasting slightly acrid, with a harsh undertone. Thuan lifted it to his lips, breathing in the trembling smell of his childhood, and thought of white grains in a bag, and Asmodeus's hand twisting his fingers away from it.

Poison.

He stared at the cup, his nostalgia thoroughly extinguished now. "You must be wondering why I'm here."

A shrug, from Kim Diep. "I'm assuming you're visiting your aunt's favourites."

She sounded she was rescuing him from embarrassment, which Thuan had admittedly not expected. He pursed his lips, then said, "I'm coming because of this." He laid, gently, the coin of the Harmony of Heaven society Hong Chi had given him.

Walking straight into traps was, admittedly, more Asmodeus's experience than his. There were times when this was the best course of action, and this was one of them.

Most of Kim Diep's face didn't move, but he saw her blink, slowly. "I'm not too sure what this is."

"A coin found on a corpse," Thuan said. He kept his voice light.

"I'm not too sure why you're coming to me."

"Ah," Thuan said. "As one of Second Aunt's… favourites, I thought you'd want to know I was looking into the matter." He shrugged. "Or rather, my husband is. He's so dreadfully bored, poor thing, and this has caught his interest."

Fortunately Asmodeus wasn't there to make forbidding faces.

"I see." Kim Diep sipped her tea, watching him for a while. "Looking to find the owner of this fine coin?" She reached out for it. Thuan didn't stop her. A thin, stubby hand wrapped around it, lifted it to the light. "It's a pretty trinket, but a rather ineffective one as currency goes."

"Certainly not at the current time," Thuan said. A sharp intake of breath from the eunuch. He went on, "It would be dreadfully inconvenient if my husband or I ran into trouble, wouldn't it? A diplomatic incident of epic proportion with a House that's nowhere as ruined or as disunited as the dragon kingdom. Hawthorn always avenges its own." He smiled, brightly.

Kim Diep was still holding the coin in front of her. She grinned, too. Thuan's message had been clear: touch him or Asmodeus, and he'd lead them straight back to her. "You're very clever," she said. "But it's just a coin, in the end. And corpses don't really have stories to tell, unless that dreadfully bored husband of yours has a way to raise the dead."

As it happened, he did. It was a costly spell and relied on the victim being a Fallen, which wasn't going to work there. Thuan debated lying about it, and decided not. It would be easy enough to see Asmodeus wasn't doing necromancy. "I'm afraid not," he said. "But he's full of surprises."

Mostly the nasty ones that came at the end of a blade when one least expected it. "Hmmm," Kim Diep said. "You're staying until the New Year is over, aren't you?"

"Family visits," Thuan said, brightly. And teachers, if Old Bao was still alive. If they all survived the next few days.

"Such an exciting time." Kim Diep smiled.

"I haven't had a proper New Year's banquet in years," Thuan said. He watched her face, carefully. "The cook in House Hawthorn does her best, but the *banh tet* just never come out tasting quite right."

"Well, I do hope you find a chance to enjoy the banquet." Kim Diep said. She used a peculiar tense, something that wasn't the future but something a great deal more uncertain. A slip of the tongue? "After it's all over, I'm sure we can find some time to walk in the gardens."

Thuan smiled. "Ah. I didn't know you enjoyed the gardens."

"I don't," Kim Diep said. "But they remind me of home."

The accent she put on the last word was too sharp and too wounding to be a coincidence. A bait he was meant to take? But the anger didn't seem feigned. "I thought home was the imperial citadel." Once taken inside the Purple Forbidden City, concubines wouldn't be allowed to leave—even after the death of the current empress they would live in her mausoleum, performing the worship of the dead.

Kim Diep laid the coin by the side of Thuan's untouched tea cup, eyes not leaving his face. "Fish yearn for the sea, and birds for the sky."

The fish and the birds were common metaphors for the concubines. "And some make their own sea and sky, don't they."

A bright smile, from Kim Diep. "Sometimes mulberry fields turn into the sea." A metaphor for profound upheavals.

"The trees die," Thuan said, sharply.

A shrug, from Kim Diep. "They die in cages anyway, don't they? Some of them have a chance, no matter how small, to take root elsewhere—drifting upwards like the banyan tree to the moon."

"Upheavals," Thuan said, swallowing bitterness on his tongue. "I see." She wanted to escape the imperial citadel and she was hoping to use the confusion to do that. "There are other ways."

A level gaze, from Kiem Diep. "I should think it's too late."

That was as good as admitting the battle lines were drawn, and no favour he could beg on her behalf from Second Aunt was going to solve anything. And her remark earlier suggested that whatever was going to happen would take place long before the banquet, which meant he was running out of time. He rose, pocketing the coin. "I see," he said, again. "Home isn't always everything you expect." Asmodeus would have pointed out she'd got there because her own family had sold her for money and status. Thuan already knew it would be cruel and pointless.

Kim Diep laughed. "Says the man who lives away from the imperial citadel."

Thuan thought of the library and the books, and the way the shelves would tower over him, a reassuring, constant thing that made sense and didn't try to utterly consume him. "I'm not saying I don't understand."

"No." Kim Diep sounded almost regretful. But then her face set again. "But it won't change anything, and we both know it. Go back to your House, child. There's still time."

But not much, not anymore.

Thuan got back to their rooms, and heard the low, steady voice of Asmodeus softly talking to someone. Someone from the kitchens he'd got to befriend? That didn't really seem in character, but why not?

He pushed open the door, and found Asmodeus in the bedoom, kneeling on the floor, quietly talking to a hunched, shivering form by the bedside table.

What in Heaven—?

It was a crab woman, and she was wearing chains linking wrists and ankles—and she'd drawn so far back into herself he could barely make out her face. She was hurt, too: the blood had dripped on the cracked tiles and the smell of it saturated the room, covering even Asmodeus's usual perfume of orange blossom and bergamot. "Asmodeus, this really isn't the time for your pleasures—"

"Ssh," Asmodeus said, barely looking up. He extended a hand towards the woman. "You can come out. I'm not going to harm you. I don't need a plaything currently."

Thuan had sharp vision, and he didn't really need much light: when the woman shifted, he saw the brand on her upper arm—an old, faded thing of cracks on the vivid orange of the carapace patches on her skin, and its matching twin on the other arm, not quite as faded but no longer red or angry, or recent. *Furtive theft.* A plaything, Asmodeus had said. "A gift," he said, aloud. Of course. A recidivist condemned to death: Second Aunt's idea of an expendable person, to keep Asmodeus sweet. Or a barbed gift from Kim Diep to betray them. "You really shouldn't—"

Anger sparkled in Asmodeus's eyes. "Be silent. You're making it worse." And, turning again to the woman. "May I?" When there was no answer, he reached out, fingers of one hand touching, lightly, the manacle on the wrist. It sprang open. The woman watched him, slowly and carefully, as he undid the other one, and the two on her ankles. "There." He held out his hand again: she still didn't move, though everything spoke of arrested flight. At length he rose; walked to the reception room under the gazes of both her and Thuan, and came back with the large tray of candied fruit and tea that had been on the table. He laid by her side, a clear offering. "Try one.

They're quite good," he said, gravely. "If you'll excuse me, I need a word with my husband here." He grabbed, seemingly absent-mindedly—except of course he seldom did anything absent-mindedly—a candied soursop which he ostentatiously nibbled on—offering permission? Telling her it wasn't poisoned? Both?

Then he turned to face Thuan.

Thuan let out the breath he wasn't aware of holding. "Not here," he said.

Asmodeus shrugged, and walked with Thuan to the reception room. Behind him, the woman was reaching out for the tray, face screwed in concentration. "You weren't far behind me."

"I take it you didn't bring her from the kitchens," Thuan said, his heart sinking.

"No. I found this delightful surprise when I opened the door. Whoever sent her our way thoughtfully added boxes of loose tea which I assume are for you, but which do have the advantage of being a little less embarrassing to deal with."

"That's not the point." Thuan's voice was more forceful than he'd thought. "You should send her back."

A raised eyebrow. "You're the squeamish one, usually."

"I don't see what that has to do with anything."

A pause. "Do you really think our mysterious benefactor would take good care of her?"

Oh. They'd kill her, or—at the very best—send her back to prison to complete her sentence. Thuan opened his mouth, closed it. "She's a condemned thief."

"I take it condemnation doesn't mean a sharp warning and told to go home and sin no more."

"It's a death penalty. Strangulation, or the slow death if the last theft was by force."

"How delightful."

"Look," Thuan said, frustrated, because he'd really wanted to have another kind of conversation and this was so not the subject he'd wanted to be tackling while exhausted. "Are we really going to be arguing about the kingdom's legal system?"

Another raised eyebrow. "I wasn't under the impression that was what we were doing." A pause. "You realise you were the one scaring her?"

"You're the one—"

"The scariest one?" His voice was grave. "In this place, in this time? You're a prince of imperial blood."

"I'm not sure I need reminding of this." Thuan looked for something to sit on, found only a high-backed, uncomfortable wooden chair. Everything smelled of mildew, and the carvings were covered in greyish algae: a familiar, almost comforting smell that was less aggressive and less sharp than Hawthorn's rotting stuffed couches.

"Because the imperial court was unpleasant for you?" Asmodeus's voice was sharp. "It doesn't change what you do to others."

How dare he? "Asmodeus—"

"Behave," Asmodeus said, sharply, which seemed completely at odds with the previous sentence. What—?

"Please." Thuan whipped round. The woman was standing against the partition screen, shivering. "Please don't send me back, my lord. They will—" She paused, then. "They will hurt me."

Asmodeus smiled, which spectacularly failed to be reassuring. "I'm not in the habit of returning gifts. What's your name?"

"Van. Cham Van, my lord." She audibly swallowed.

"You're not helping," Thuan said. And Asmodeus didn't care one jot for Van, either.

"And neither are you. This is really not the time for grandstanding."

"Grandstanding? You're being unpleasant."

"That's generally what I do, yes. Why don't you go have a look at the tea to see if we know who sent it? It's on the bedside table." It was imperious enough not to be a question, and Thuan was halfway to the table before he realised it and stopped. Asmodeus had turned to Van, "Why are you here?"

An expansive shrug. "I didn't pick. They grabbed me and left me here, my lord."

Asmodeus watched her for a while, face cocked. "Thief," he said, finally.

"My lord." She didn't look up, or offer anything more.

"You're worried about Thuan. I can assure you he's not going to judge you."

Thuan was, in fact, feeling very much like he wanted to leave altogether, but demons take him if he followed Asmodeus's strongly worded suggestion. He settled for going into the bedroom and going fishing for the tray of candied fruit. Coconut, lotus seeds, papaya... he grabbed a lotus seed and sat down in a chair—and finally found himself drifting towards the boxes of tea.

They'd been aligned on his side of the bed—just as the woman—Van—had been on Asmodeus's side of the bed. If nothing else, that had been pointed. He couldn't see a message or a crest: rummaging didn't seem to yield anything much, except that the tea was of mediocre quality, the leaves far too large and with an astringency he could almost taste. Hong Chi or Second Aunt would have access to something better.

By the time Asmodeus came out of the room, Thuan had come to a not wholly pleasant decision. "I think it's from the society. A, ah. Distraction. Or a bribe."

"I'm finding the whole murder investigation entertaining enough, unfortunately for them," Asmodeus said. "And seriously, boxes of tea? They price you quite low."

Thuan raised an eyebrow, and stopped himself from saying anything about the worth of a person's life in the presence of Van. She was behind Asmodeus—she was busy bandaging the last of her wounds with a patch of embroidered cloth that looked suspiciously like one of Thuan's shirts. When she was done, she looked up, throwing Thuan a glance that was filled with fear, a split second before she seemed to remember something and relax.

Thuan had the unpleasant suspicion that it was

Asmodeus's frank admission that he wouldn't find her death entertaining enough. "We don't need a hanger on," he said, stiffly.

"You haven't even asked what she stole." Asmodeus sounded chirpy and cheerful, with that wide smile suggesting he was seconds from driving the knife in.

Thuan didn't really like being on *that* end of the blade.

A pause that was all for show, then: "It was rice," Asmodeus said.

Thuan opened his mouth, closed it.

Van said, in the silence, "The barriers around my town didn't get their spells renewed, so the currents didn't flow the right way for growing rice." She spread her hands, wincing when her bandages shifted. "The officials at the tribunal said there was no money for repairs, but the seedlings all came up rotted through and through, and I didn't know what else to do. My mother and my wife were starving to death. Your highness," she said, almost as an afterthought.

It was wrong to steal. He'd been told, over and over, by a succession of tutors at home and then later in the imperial citadel, that honesty and loyalty were the foundations of a society. That stealing was against the order of things; but worse than that, that it was utterly unnecessary because everyone was provided for. That thought clashed, in his mind, with Van's white face, utterly drained of blood. She was looking straight at him, with none of the reverence he'd expect—but she was braced for him to strike her down.

"It takes time," he said, finally, and felt terrible, because time wasn't going to give her rice, or make her family better. He leant against a chair, opened his mouth to say none of this was helping, and then realised how utterly self-centred and callous that made him seem. "It shouldn't have happened to you or your town." And if he had any say in it, he was going to have a rather sharp word with Hong Chi.

Van didn't move, but she visibly relaxed. Asmodeus laid a hand on her shoulder, squeezing briefly. "You're staying here for the time being." And, to Thuan, "I'm satisfied she has absolutely no idea of what's going on."

Thuan's heart sank when he saw that Asmodeus had absolutely no intention of sending Van out of the room. "Look, I get that it's a hard and unfair time for her, but really, what we're doing is confidential—"

"Oh, she knows she shouldn't blab or I'll cut out her tongue." Asmodeus's voice was matter of fact. He looked entirely too smug.

Thuan said, coldly, "Are you done lashing at me? Because *my* bribe wasn't a person to torture to death, and last I checked half of Paris was starving, so it's not like you have any claim to moral superiority."

"You misunderstand. This isn't about moral superiority."

Probably not, which made it worse. It was merely his seeing open wounds and unable to resist pushing where it hurt, for all his professions of caring earlier. Thuan should have known better than to trust his husband—he really,

really should, but it hurt all the same. "Fine. Do you want to discuss the actual investigation?"

"The concubine." Asmodeus's voice was sharp.

"Well, the good news is that if I was placing bets, I'd definitely put a lot of strings of cash on Kim Diep being not only aware, but in charge of the plot."

"So your cousin isn't completely out of touch. Good. Anything else?"

"Other than her knowing we're onto her?" Thuan shrugged. "It's going to happen before the banquet. Long before, I think."

"Is that a bet?"

"A less… certain one. And I know some of the way she feels, so whatever it is will cause massive disruptions in the citadel, which doesn't really narrow down the field."

"Mmm." Asmodeus looked thoughtful. "What I learnt in the kitchens is mostly that it's nothing to do with the kitchens. That powder in the pouch doesn't poison food."

"Let me guess, you know this because you tried it on someone."

"Close, but no. No one had seen a similar powder, but we fed it to one of the pets—those salamanders that are everywhere in the citadel."

"So the powder doesn't do anything?"

"I didn't say *that*. As an unguent, or a blood contaminant, it might still have nasty properties. I handed it to Madeleine."

Madeleine was House Hawthorn's alchemist, and she'd come with their delegation looking rather more enthusiastic than usual. She'd barricaded herself in with Véronique and Xuan Thao, two of Second Aunt's aides, excitedly comparing alchemy and the stasis *khi*-water spells, and they had all looked rather unlikely to emerge, even for the promise of a festival banquet.

"All right," Thuan said, grudgingly. "If anyone knows how to make powder talk, it'll be Véronique, Xuan Thao and her."

"I have faith in that, if nothing else," Asmodeus said. "Everyone agrees Ai Linh probably picked up the pouch somewhere outside of the kitchens. She was really preoccupied the last few days, though. It's quite likely she was making up her mind to denounce whoever she'd taken it from."

"Except they caught up with her first." Thuan fingered the coin in his sleeves. "That still leaves a lot of options, though." The citadel was gearing up for New Year, and a lot of ceremonies were taking place at the same time: even living in the citadel Thuan had barely been able to keep up with them, and he half-suspected a host of planners at the Ministry of Rites were the only ones who knew all of these at once.

"I did find this in the pouch," Asmodeus said. He produced, like a conjurer out of a hat, a single pinkish petal.

Thuan stared at it. "It's a flower," he said, finally. "In the gardens?"

"Don't look at me," Asmodeus said. "I was rather hoping you'd be able to identify it. I'm not a gardening person."

"Neither am I!"

In the silence, it was Van who spoke. "It's a celestial pearl lily. My lord. It only grows in the imperial gardens."

"Oh, drop the 'my lord'. I'm not ruling anything that's relevant to you, and neither is he," Thuan said, and glared at Asmodeus, daring him to speak up.

A smile. "I disagree, since I currently hold her life."

Thuan opened his mouth, closed it. It was either that or having someone else hold it, wasn't it? "Fine," he said. "If she stays with us, it's not on those terms."

Thuan fished in his sleeves, and located a Hawthorn tracker disk, which he held out to Van.

Asmodeus raised an eyebrow. "Really?"

Thuan didn't care. "That's the membership and protection of House Hawthorn. It's not my husband's caprice or good will. It's a promise that if you stand by the House, we'll stand by you, even after this is over. By you and by your family." He paused, then, realising that made him little better than Asmodeus. "And if that includes your ultimately leaving the House and going back into the dragon kingdom or elsewhere, we can do that, too."

Van swallowed. She looked at Asmodeus—who shrugged, nonchalant and pleasant, but he was angry. He'd had plans for her, and they'd probably included toying with her more, enjoying her fear and uncertainty, something her being a House dependent would prevent— because both he and Thuan would then have obligations to her.

Well, tough luck. Thuan wasn't going to roll over and

let decency fly out the window that easily. And he knew Asmodeus hated losing face.

At length, Asmodeus nodded. "Take it," he said. "If you want."

"My lord…"

"Thuan is right." A shrug. "I always stand by my dependents."

Van reached out, lightning-fast, her hand lengthening into pincers—she'd slipped the tracker disk around her neck almost before Thuan could even move. The disk fused to her skin: it held a magical spell that would let both Thuan and Asmodeus know where she was. She looked at them both, uncertainly.

Thuan said, "We're also going to need the name of your birth town, and of your mother and wife, to see if we can track her down."

"Tam Phong, in Anh Sang province. Her name is Old Vi. Tran Thi Hanh Vi. My wife is Le Thi Hai Yen."

Thuan nodded. "I can't make promises on this," he said. "But I'll ask after this is over."

"Thank you, my lord," Van said. "Sorry."

Asmodeus laughed. "Actually, you'll find that becoming a dependent of the House does make us your lords, so this is entirely correct this time." He still sounded angry, but at least it wasn't at her. Not that he'd take back the disk from her: Asmodeus's backstabbing was entirely reserved for outsiders to the House, and occasionally Thuan when he was particularly angry. Another bridge they'd cross when they got around to it.

Thuan spared a brief prayer to his ancestors to let Second Aunt find about this *after* they'd thwarted the secret society—or after the dynasty went down, even. Anything but the excoriating talking down she'd give him for taking one of her subjects without her permission: not only disloyalty to a ruler but more importantly disloyalty to an elder. "Let's go find the gardens," he said.

There were two locations in the gardens where the celestial pearl lily grew, as it turned out: one of them in the Empress Dowager's gardens, and they emphatically didn't want outsiders coming in.

"You must request permission from the Ministry of Rites," a rather stuck-up dragon of the first rank said, drawing herself to her full height. Behind her were four other guards in lacquered uniforms. The gardens themselves were at the back of the citadel, behind a wall of stone behind a coral reef: a double line of defense with a single wide, circular door in the shape of a longevity symbol, in front of which Thuan, Asmodeus and Van were currently stuck.

"I could ask the Empress Dowager," Thuan said, smiling through gritted teeth, the antlers and scales of his dragon form shimmering into existence on his face—along with the sharp canines and pointed teeth in the huge maw. He'd seen his maternal grandmother briefly on arriving. She had taken to Asmodeus, whom she found decisive and rather sweet: the first was understandable,

41

the second one was just deuced odd—though Asmodeus, who had looked up her bloodthirsty empress days, thoroughly approved of her.

"Certainly not," the dragon official said. "The Dowager is resting, to get all the strength she needs for New Year's Eve."

Asmodeus looked as though he was going to stab the dragon and walk over her corpse, which would definitely *not* improve anything. Thuan opened his mouth, but Van got in first, "It's Tet," she said, bowing low. She was now wearing loose purple robes that covered both the brands on her arms. They were lightly embroidered along the hem and the sleeves: to all intents and purposes, Van looked indistinguishable from a minor official of the ninth rank. The dragon looked at her as if she'd been dragged in with the trash, but visibly softened when she bowed all the way to the ground with practiced ease. "This is a time for honouring family and the ancestors. His Highness would merely like to make a filial gesture for his grandmother. He knows that she loves langsats, and there is a grove of three langsat trees in this corner of the gardens which fruit out of season."

The dragon official looked at the guards. They shrugged. At length one of them said, "The back of the garden is a bit temporally disjointed, and there are langsat trees there. It may not be safe, though. Your Highness," she said, bowing to Thuan.

"Mmm." The dragon official looked at Van, and then at Thuan.

Van bowed even lower. "You wouldn't want to stand in the way of filial piety, would you? It would be so distressing to His Highness to have to face his grandmother empty-handed, when he owes her so much."

Thuan kept his face straight, and sent a tendril of magic on Asmodeus's lips to be sure that he wouldn't say anything.

At length, the dragon official shook her head. "You and your retainer can go in," she said to Thuan. She pointed to Asmodeus. "*He* stays here. No foreigners."

"Charmed," Asmodeus said, mockingly bowing to her. "I'll find profitable ways to spend the time, no doubt."

"Behave," Thuan said.

"Oh, I'll be sure to do so, being bereft of gifts," Asmodeus said, sharply. Thuan didn't rise to the jibe. He walked between the spears of the guards, into the Dowager Queen's gardens, with Van following behind him.

The gardens were a long expanse of algae and sea grass, leading up to a pavilion on a rocky spur overlooking a basin full of opalescent pebbles—the pavillion's sloped roof had cracked longevity tiles and lacquered pillars invaded by greyish mould. In the distance were the citadel's walls, separating them from the capital's busier streets. The noises from the city were faint, the din of marketplaces and street sellers almost inaudible. Overhead, the sky was grey, and the sunlight the dappled and shivering one of a star seen through water. Shoals of fish wheeled above them, light glistening on their scales. The grass was dry, breaking under Thuan's feet. He couldn't see amphibians or crabs.

"Thank you for the intervention," Thuan said. "You weren't a farmer, were you? In your town."

"A farmer." Van looked puzzled. "Oh, you thought that because I knew about the celestial pearl lily. Goodness, no. I was a clerk in the county tribunal. That's why I ended up in the capital for my execution."

As a convicted official. "The magistrate you worked for—"

"—denounced me." Van looked sick, as pale and withdrawn as she'd been when he'd first met her. "It was… unpleasant."

Something twisted in Thuan's chest. "You don't have to explain further. I'm sorry. I have a lot of baggage from my time in the citadel, and it turns out a lot of it isn't pleasant or decent."

Van shrugged, her patches of broken carapace glistening in the light. "You're of imperial blood."

That didn't make it better, not one bit. "Yes. And it's not an excuse and no one should use it as such." But he had, hadn't he? His blood was the reason he'd made it out of the court at all—unlike Kim Diep or Van.

All the coral formations and algae-covered rocks looked suspiciously like each other, and the profusion of colourful sea anemones and aquatic flowers just blurred into insignificance. Thuan withdrew the petal from his sleeve again, stared at it. "Celestial pearl lily. Any idea what the actual plant would look like?"

Van's face was a study in neutrality. "I've only seen diagrams, but I think it's quite similar to some of the other water lilies. Here." She pointed to a patch of leaves and algae by the pond's edge that looked like nothing so much as the other patches—except that, getting closer, Thuan saw small pinkish flowers scattered in the midst of them.

"All right." He looked up: there were a handful of gardeners and officials around, but due to its limited access it was otherwise a very quiet place. "They're way smaller than I thought."

"And that's a problem?"

"Well, they're sickly and not very impressive." Shriveling a beautiful and symbolic patch of plants or anemones in the Empress Dowager's gardens—the progenitor of the current empress and the symbol of the continuity of bloodlines—would have been a statement. Not as clearcut of one as he'd hoped, but… "You could take them all out and barely anyone would notice."

Van said, "Can I ask a question?"

"Of course," Thuan said, startled. "You don't need to ask permission."

"Can you tell me exactly what the investigation is?" A grimace. "I got some of it from your conversations, but…"

Thuan hesitated. Hong Chi would never forgive him for sharing her confidences. But Van looked entirely sincere, and for all his faults Asmodeus was an excellent judge of character. "Trying to prevent… an incident." He summarised, quickly, what Hong Chi had told him.

"Saving the dynasty." Van's voice was carefully neutral.

"Yes," Thuan said. He paused, then. "I realise these are the same people who condemned you to death."

Van stared at him for a while. "No. They're not." It was final, something he wasn't meant to probe into. And then, in a smaller voice, "I want to live, my lord. I want my family to be safe." She sounded ashamed.

Thuan wished, paradoxically, that Asmodeus were there. "We protect our own," he said. "Asmodeus is right: he doesn't much care about what you stole."

"But you do." Van's voice was sharp.

"I did." Thuan sighed. "Not my best moment, admittedly."

Van looked shocked. "My lord—"

"You'll find I don't much care about whether I'm losing face."

"But you care about this," Van said, slowly.

"It's a family affair," Thuan said—something she could surely see the appeal of.

Van closed her eyes, for a brief moment. "What you said about finding my mother and my wife—"

"We'll make it happen," Thuan said. Hong Chi was going to owe him by the time they were done, and it was an easy thing to leverage. "We're not abandoning you or your family. That's how the House works: we always stand by our own."

Van relaxed a fraction. "When this is over."

"Yes," Thuan said, as firmly and decisively as he could. "Things are going to be very different for us as well when we're done. The Court will owe us, and it'll be much easier to get our way. All we have to do is navigate until then."

"Navigate." Van put a particular accent on the word, one that Thuan didn't quite know how to interpret.

"It'll be ok," he said. "I realise you're in a very vulnerable position right now."

"I should be dead." Van's voice was flat.

Thuan sighed. "I can't change that. But Asmodeus and I can make sure that you're always in our sight. Does that help?"

Van said nothing for a while. "In a way." She didn't sound wholly convinced, but then why would she trust them?

Thuan said, "You don't know us yet. Give us a chance. Please." Which was a tall order given Asmodeus's earlier statements.

Bitter laughter. "It's not as though I have much of a choice." And then, before Thuan could say anything else, "I'll help you, my lord."

Thuan felt acutely embarrassed, and cast about for another thing to say. "Let's just get this done, shall we?"

Van nodded.

"I could freeze all of these flowers to death, and no one would even notice anything was missing from the gardens. Are they used for something specific, maybe?"

Van's face screwed in thought. "I can't remember what the diagram said—"

The wind had changed: it blew into Thuan's face the

smell of brine undercut with mildew. And something else, too, a sharp and animal smell he'd have known anywhere. "Wait."

A little bit further on, there was a patch of coral reefs overlooking a smaller pavilion decorated with images of Immortals and peach flowers, where someone had left a sheet of paper bearing calligraphy in a beautiful hand, as well as the vermillion imprint of a seal: it wasn't one of the official ones of the dynasty, the ones under lock and key in a stronghold of the citadel, but rather the personal one of the Empress Dowager.

"My lord?" Van asked, but Thuan was already foraging at the bottom of the reef.

"Here," he said, unfolding what had been stuffed between two corals: the long robes of an official, soaked in blood. The smell was now unbearably strong: he fought the urge to throw the robes away from him. They were much larger than the ones Ai Linh had been wearing, and in any case Ai Linh wouldn't have been allowed to access the Dowager's gardens.

"There's no body anywhere," Van said. She frowned. "Wait."

There *was* no body, but there was a rather suspicious looking charred zone, and blackened ivory fragments Van lifted to the light. "Bones." She sounded matter of fact: Thuan felt rather less chirpy about it. Not about the body itself: he'd seen his share of them, but the fact that someone had just committed murder a few meters away from his grandmother.

"So they killed someone and they burnt the body. It's deuced odd no one realised there was a missing person." The burning of the body could have been magical, which would have generated no smoke, and he supposed the wind was blowing the wrong way, which explained why no one had smelled the blood: Thuan and Asmodeus were both unusually sensitive to the smell.

"They might have reported it but been unable to find them," Van said. "It's not like they would notify you in particular, would they?" She grimaced. "Not many bones left." She lifted up a fragment of antlers. "Dragon, quite probably, but I'm not even sure what sex."

"Mmm." Thuan shook the tunic loose, stared at it. "Uh. They slit the throat." All the blood was coming from the neck. The patch on the chest bore the attributes of the fourth rank and the mark of the Ministry of Rites, but there was no other indication of affiliation. Under the patch was the hard smooth surface of something, and a jolt of *khi*-water up his fingers. "Ah. A sort of tracker spell. That's why they didn't hit the chest. Or burn the clothes."

"That's reserved for just a few departments," Van said. "The critical ones."

Of course. Thuan sighed. He looked, again, at the pavilion. A quiet, personal spot. "I'm going to need to check a few things. How much *khi*-magic do you know?"

In the end, Van was the more expert magic-wielder: Thuan was mostly a theoretician with a good eye for detail, and he let her check every single patch around the pavilion from the lacquered pillars to the coral reefs and the scattering of algae. She shrugged, finally. "Nothing wrong I can see, apart from the usual spells of protection on the pavilion. I'm not Ministry of Rites, though."

"No." Thuan stared at the pavilion again. He'd bunched the tunic under the folds of his, and he was acutely aware of the way that the blood was seeping into his own clothes. "Neither am I." He bit his lips. "It mostly sounds like this was a convenient spot for a murder. It's not too difficult to access, comparatively speaking, and it's secluded. I'm sure the Empress's private palace has emptier gardens, but it's all but impossible to get into that."

"All right," Van said. "But who?"

"If only I knew." Looking only at the offices which had tracker spells and access to the Dowager Empress's gardens would thin the ranks of victims, but it was a fallacy Thuan wouldn't fall prey to. The murderer could very easily have been the one with access. "Maybe Asmodeus will have better ideas when he sees the tunic. He's usually the one with the murder skills."

A smodeus, of course, wasn't anywhere near the entrance to the gardens when Thuan and Van came out. "He's with the Dowager Empress," the dragon official said, looking bored.

"He—what?"

"One of her servants came inquiring for something and saw him there, and extended an invitation to him."

In other words, grabbed him and not let go. Thuan

winced. Grandmother had liked Asmodeus, but that was on the basis of a short meal and small talk through an interpreter. They'd been in the garden for way longer than that. "Let's go get him before he manages to outstay his welcome."

They were halfway to the Empress Dowager's quarters, walking along a pillared corridor, when a voice called out. "Your Highness!"

It was someone Thuan didn't know, a dragon official of the fifth rank who carried himself with the arrogance of someone newly raised to the office. "We haven't been introduced," he said, coldly.

"Oh, my name is Dang Quang," the official said. "I'm the prefect of Dai An."

It was a faraway province which wasn't very familiar to Thuan. "If you'll excuse me," he said, hardening his voice. "I've got other pressing business to deal with."

Dang Quang moved—seemingly innocently, but ending up in Thuan's way all the same. "Oh, I won't hold you long, your Highness. I just wanted to make sure you hadn't been deceived."

Nice bait, but Thuan wasn't biting. "I'm three hundred years old and not a naive innocent anymore." He was about to add another blistering remark, when he noticed Van's uncanny silence. Turning, briefly, he saw she was holding herself straight, knuckles white and much too close to Thuan—using him as a shield. "You're Van's old superior," he said. "The former magistrate of Tam Phong."

"I had that honour."

He needed to get Van out as soon as possible, but he also needed to make sure that Dang Quang wasn't going to come back into her life anymore. "Talk," he said, curtly.

Dang Quang smiled. "She's a thief and a liar, your Highness, and she'll betray you as she betrayed me."

"Hmm," Thuan said. "She serves a use. And she's mine now, *child*." He deliberately used a pronoun he was entitled to use, but which emphasized Dang Quang's vastly inferior status.

A pause. Dang Quang said, "She should be dead."

Ah. That kind of man, vindictive in addition to being a sadist. On second thought... magistrate of a county to prefect was a rather sharp and unusual promotion, which probably meant he'd risen on the strength of something. Thuan would have bet anti-corruption, with Van as one of his prize achievements, one of his own clerks caught stealing from the state and afforded no favour due to her position. So not only a victim he didn't want to let go of, but a symbol of his former life he'd want eradicated.

Great.

Thuan said, softly, "She's what I want her to be. No more, no less. And you should really consider whether you want to make enemies of us."

Dang Quang smiled. "I have always acted in respect of the First Teacher's rules, your Highness. My loyalty to the state is unquestioned."

A not particularly subtle threat, but then it didn't need to be. Thuan and Asmodeus weren't exactly on very firm ground by taking one of the empire's own subjects and binding her to their House—and a condemned criminal overdue punishment at that.

Thuan raised an eyebrow, with a confidence he didn't particularly feel. "Let's test, this, shall we? Care to come with me see the Dowager Empress?"

It was a bluff, but it worked. Dang Quang grimaced. "Far be it from me to stand between you and your grandmother, your Highness. But I'll respectfully keep inquiring about the proper course of action."

"Of course," Thuan said—and watched him go, heart sinking. He made sure that Dang Quang was completely out of sight before he grabbed Van and marched her into a secluded alcove, and held her until the shaking of her body vanished—because it wouldn't exactly have been seemly to be hugging one's own retainer in the context of the imperial citadel.

"My lord…" Van looked as though she was going to be sick.

"Ssssh," Thuan said. "You all right?"

"No," Van said. "But you really shouldn't involve yourself—"

"Don't," Thuan said. He released her, and leant against the carvings of the wall, breathing hard. "That's the way it goes. House rules." Or at any rate the ones he and Asmodeus had made for themselves. A belated thought came to him. "And let me know if I should be touching you the next time. I'm sorry, I should have asked first and I panicked when I saw how white you looked."

Van looked as though she didn't know what to say

anymore. Thuan laughed, with a carelessness he very much didn't feel. "Consent," he said. "It's not a word I take lightly. And Dang Quang isn't going to touch you anymore. It'd be war between House Hawthorn and the kingdom if he did."

"You wouldn't—"

"I might not," Thuan said. "But Asmodeus would."

"Your husband—"

Thuan sighed. "I get it. He's aggressive and he threatened you and he's generally very, very unpleasant. But he's also very difficult to shake off when it comes to the well-being of his people."

Van looked doubtful.

"You'll see," Thuan said. And then, because he had to, "Is Dang Quang likely to hurt your mother or your wife?"

Van shook her head. "All his issues are with me, and it's harder to look like a good official if you touch old women or lesser spouses."

"Ah." Thuan said. He wasn't sure if that made it better or worse.

Worse, probably.

The Empress Dowager's quarters were further into the citadel, a palace accessed through a huge recessed courtyard, and then a huge flight of stairs leading to a platform where one waited to be picked up by a eunuch or one of the Dowager's handpicked servants. The palace itself was entered through a pillared entrance, the reception room vast and airy, a long embroidered carpet leading to a throne at the back of the room, everything carved in what had once been white stone but was now bluish or greyish. Thuan could have taken on his full dragon shape and not even touched the distant ceiling, and there was barely a trace of mildew anywhere: not because it didn't grow, but because an army of servants would have removed it.

The Empress Dowager was sitting on the steps in front of the regal chair she was meant to be occupying, propped up on embroidered cushions and nibbling on a dumpling Asmodeus had just handed her. He was kneeling on the other side of a low lacquered table loaded with food, which looked extensively sampled—and he was probably the only person who could pull off kneeling without seeming submissive.

"Ah, husband," Asmodeus said, laying down his chopsticks near a bowl of sautéed cucumbers. "How good of you to join us."

"Grandmother," Thuan said, and bowed. "Husband." He wasn't going to bow, and in any case he was reasonably sure he was the eldest in the couple. "I trust you had a good time." Behind him, Van had prostrated herself; when she got up, she took up a silent kneeling position a pace behind Asmodeus.

"Very good," Grandmother said. "Your husband was just telling me about the interrogations he'd led in the Court of Persuasion." She looked like a sweet, forgetful old dragon, her antlers translucent, her eyes rheumy and unfocused, the scales on her cheeks and the back of her hands lustreless—and perhaps she was forgetful those days, but she hadn't risen to marry Thuan's grandfather

55

through smiles. Thuan had it on good authority—hers, in fact—that she'd murdered about five concubines to get noticed by the then-Emperor, and executed quite a few more to keep the peace in the six chambers.

"What a delightful conversation," Thuan said. "If you'll excuse me, Asmodeus and I really need to get going."

Grandmother patted one of the cushions next to her. "So fast? Come, come, tell me about your time in the citadel. You must be finding it so dreadfully boring."

In fact, Thuan had about reached his upper limit of excitement. When he moved past Asmodeus, Asmodeus's gaze rose, sharply, towards him, his mouth shaping a single word. *Blood?*

Yes, Thuan said, and sat down next to Grandmother and dearly hoped that her sense of smell had weakened with age. "It's changed," he said, finally, casting about for subjects of conversation that wouldn't be about impending rebellion or the mandate of Heaven or anything that would involve breaking Hong Chi's confidence.

A silence. Grandmother considered him, unfocused eyes turned towards his face. Her perfume of sandalwood and cedar floated to him, sweet and familiar. "*You* have changed."

On second thought, perhaps he'd have preferred to be grilled about the rebellion.

"He has," Asmodeus said. He sounded smug. "Fortunately, he's learnt to be a little more ruthless."

"Ha! I bet you're still the ruthless one," Grandmother said.

"Touché." He bowed to her, with a mocking smile. "Thuan is the bookish one."

"Books are such useful resources," Grandmother said. "Our ancestors were nowhere as squeamish as the court these days." A snort. "Would you believe they only exile traitorous officials those days?"

"An awful waste of lives that could be spectacularly taken," Asmodeus said.

Van, who'd remained kneeling behind Asmodeus, was shivering. Thuan cast about for a change of conversation. "Traitorous officials. So there's much unrest in some ministries those days, then?"

A snort from Grandmother. "The Ministry of Rites is a shambles. Particularly the Court of Imperial Sacrifices. Not only can they not keep track of their own personnel, but they can't keep them in line anymore, it seems."

The ones in charge of the large and small acts of state worship. Thuan frowned. "I hope the lineage is still properly worshipped?"

"Of course, of course."

"That's such a shame," Thuan said, brightly. "About the personnel. You'd think people could be better disciplined."

"Hmmmf," Grandmother said. "People kept vanishing or coming back at inopportune times. Gone home to mourn a relative or for New Year's, they said. Easier to say this than admit the Ministry didn't keep track of their own people." She picked a dumpling from the table, held it out to him. "Eat. You look thin and over worried. That's not good for you. You should have children."

Asmodeus's mouth closed on whatever cutting remark he'd been about to make. Thuan would have had much greater joy in Asmodeus's discomfiture if he hadn't been at the forefront of said discomfiture. "We'll think about it," he said.

Van looked uncomfortable. Thuan couldn't blame her. He grabbed the dumpling and ate it, washing it down with tea and hoping to Heaven Grandmother wasn't about to follow this up with another remark in the same vein. "Thank you," he said. "We'll come and visit you again before the New Year?"

"Please," Grandmother said. "I always enjoy hearing from my grandchildren, and your husband is such a sweet delight."

The sweet, murderous delight rose and bowed gravely to Grandmother, and they made their way out of the Empress Dowager's quarters in silence, with Van a few paces behind them.

At least it wasn't a major diplomatic incident.

"So," Asmodeus said, when they were back in their quarters. "Blood?"

Thuan withdrew the tunic from under his clothes. His under robes were soaked: fortunately he'd been wearing the full five-panel dress and it had only touched the under layers. He threw it on the floor of the reception room. "Van can explain where we found it. I'm going to put on some other clothes."

When he came out of the bedroom—wearing red robes embroidered with dragons that felt too pretentious—Asmodeus had spread the suit out, and was examining it with Fallen magic, Van silently watching him.

At length he rose. "It's soaked with arterial blood, but then again given the neck area it was quite likely the severing of the carotid artery caused the death. Van said the bones you found were a dragon's." It wasn't a question.

"Mmm," Thuan said. "A nameless dragon official of the fourth rank who was brought there and killed."

"And that's your only lead? That's... thin."

"A little more than tea and dumplings with my grandmother," Thuan said, sharply.

"It was delightful tea," Asmodeus said. "She has scintillating conversation."

"Reminiscing about everyone she's tortured to death?"

"Precisely."

Van said, "You asked the question about the ministries on purpose. Didn't you?"

"Yes," Thuan said. "And I got my answer. A court in shambles is a great way to 'lose' someone. I think we should check there for the owner of this tunic." He paused, but he couldn't leave Asmodeus out of the other thing. "I also need to talk to you. Alone."

Asmodeus smiled. "Of course."

They moved to the bedroom. Asmodeus leant against the wall, smiling. "Is this the part where you beg for my forgiveness?"

"What?"

"For stealing Van."

"You didn't need Van."

"I beg to differ. One source of entertainment doesn't preclude another." A smile, and an invisible touch of magic on both of Thuan's cheeks, slowly descending towards his lips and briefly holding there, like a finger silencing him. "Fortunately, I have a few ideas on how you can make it up to me."

"Now isn't the time."

The same touch of magic pinned both his arms at his sides, and stroked, again and again, his earlobes and the base of his neck. "Asmodeus—" he said, struggling to move—or to breathe, as the touch circled his chest, pinching again and again, slowly descending along his spine.

Asmodeus kissed him. It felt like coming up for air for the briefest of moments, inhaling the heady perfume of orange blossom and bergamot—before the magical touch all started again and desire, unbearable and sharp, rose—he turned his lips up again, for another kiss, struggling to sort out his thoughts, to seek or want anything other than the fire that seemed to be engulfing all of it.

Abruptly, it stopped; and he stood, panting, in the middle of the bedroom, with Asmodeus back where he'd been, leaning against the wall with a mocking smile on his face. "You—" Thuan said.

"Oh, I'm not heartless." Asmodeus smiled. "Not *totally*. But you do deserve to be left hanging for a while, after what you pulled off with Van."

Thuan closed his eyes, trying to find thoughts—any

coherent thoughts that wouldn't be a primal scream of frustration. "I'd very much appreciate another form of retribution next time," he finally managed. "Also, we have a problem."

Asmodeus raised an eyebrow.

"His name is Dang Quang, and he wants Van back."

"Back?" Asmodeus's eyebrow went higher. "Really, he doesn't know either of us very well."

"Mmm," Thuan said. "But he knows how the imperial court works, and that we're not exactly on very solid ground. And I don't know what he did to Van, but—"

"You can guess, surely," Asmodeus said.

"You're not guessing." Thuan's voice was sharp.

"No. The clothes she was wearing when she arrived are quite flimsy—" he sounded clinical, but then again he wasn't attracted to women in the slightest, and for all that he enjoyed people's pain, his idea of sex was mutual consent—"and I have a good eye for wounds." His gaze was harsh, not admirative. Really, really bad, then.

"Do you think I need the details?" Thuan asked.

"Mmm." Asmodeus considered him. "No. You'd get angry, and next thing I know you'd be hauling Dang Quang in front of the Empress. Come on, let's go see Van."

Thuan didn't really know if Van had eavesdropped on them—he didn't think so, because she'd busied herself with the tunic: she'd taken a paper and a brush from the large reception room table and was busy sketching.

"What's this?" Asmodeus asked.

"Body-shape," Van said.

"From a tunic?"

"They're a court official," Van said. "They'll have had it tailored. It's practically compulsory. The state will provide the seal of the office, for passing orders, and they will also provide mass-produced robes, but everyone wants to personalise their rank patches to look like more powerful officials, and there's so much gold and silver that can be worked into clothes while still following official dressing code, if you have a good tailor."

"We could ask the tailors, then," Asmodeus said.

"We could, but we'd need to narrow it down. There's too many of them in the capital." She bit her lip. Thuan couldn't help but notice she wasn't scared of Asmodeus when she was in her element.

Van finished annotating her sketch, and laid it on the table. "There. It's quite a large person."

Asmodeus and Thuan bent over it at the same time— Thuan's antlers tangling, briefly, with Asmodeus's hair. "That's unusual but hardly extraordinary," Asmodeus said.

Van said, "They had visible shoulder spurs, and they weren't very wealthy. The cloth is distended on the shoulder-line. There are ways to accommodate this, but they cost money."

Asmodeus raised an eyebrow. "Observant."

Van shrugged. "I've been a civil servant for a while." Her hands became pincers for a brief moment. "And it's not always convenient for a crab either. Carapace does tend to make a mess of clothes."

"I don't imagine they keep records of officials by size or by visible features," Asmodeus said.

"No," Thuan said. "From what Grandmother was saying, it's possibly a miracle if they've kept records at all."

"Hmm." Asmodeus weighed the sketch, staring at it, for a while. "I'm going to ask again. How much does this all mean to you?"

Thuan looked up, chilled. "What do you mean?"

"You're upset by each new discovery on this case. And Van feels unsafe, which is unfair to her."

"So you just want us to give up?"

"I want us to return to Hawthorn," Asmodeus said. "After a detour to track down Van's mother and wife and make sure they're safe, too."

"Van agreed to help us."

"Did she?"

"Why don't we ask her? Van?"

Van looked from one of them to the other, her face white. "My lords..." Thuan remembered what they'd told each other, her doubts, her carefully phrased neutrality. Not contradicting him, because he was her head of House. How could he have missed it?

Asmodeus laughed, and it was low-pitched and wounding. "You're asking her to choose between her two masters. See what I mean about unfair?"

"But you're not being fairer."

"I know about fear," Asmodeus said, simply. And, to

Van, "You'd give anything to be away from Dang Quang, wouldn't you." It wasn't a question.

Van didn't say anything. Thuan remembered how white she'd been, how much she'd shaken in his grip. "We're not defined by what we fear," he said.

"But sometimes fear becomes all that we are." Asmodeus moved away from Van, putting the sketch on the bedtime table. "A sign you should either stab the cause of such fears in the throat or run away and regroup."

"And stab it in the throat when you're ready? That's not a way to live."

"That's mine." Asmodeus's voice was sharp. "I don't complain too much about yours. It'd behoove you to do the same."

"You don't care about me," Van said, in the silence, to Asmodeus. "He said—"

"Thuan?" Asmodeus smiled.

Van swallowed. "No, that's not what I wanted to say. Thuan said I'd understand you didn't mean it. All of the… unpleasantness. But… you'd have killed me, earlier. For pleasure."

"Ah. I might have, but Thuan changed the terms by binding you to the House." Asmodeus looked at her, for a while. He moved closer to her, his hand resting, lightly, on her pendant: the disk with the arms of House Hawthorn engraved on it, the hawthorn tree circled by a crown. "This," he said, "is a promise. It means that you don't feel terrified or unsafe. Your enemies do."

"Terrified. Of you."

"Of course. Do you see anyone getting terrified of Thuan?" His face became serious again. "You're one of ours, now. I'll let harm come to me before it comes to you. Do you believe that?"

Van stared at him. Then—and it must have cost all she had—"You can't be choosing me over your husband."

"Considering what Dang Quang will do if he gets hold of you? Yes. Thuan will be mildly uncomfortable—"

"By such trivialities as my entire family exterminated?" It was the wrong thing to say, but Thuan couldn't help himself anymore.

A raised eyebrow. "Preventing this from happening is Hong Chi's job, and she's managed to dump it on you by appealing to your guilt. Don't get sentimental."

How could he? "I'm not getting sentimental!"

"True." Asmodeus's face didn't move. "You're getting annoyed. And still feeling guilty." A sigh. He moved a fraction closer to Thuan. "Your cousin is playing you like a fiddle, and not a particularly good one. You're not the one who got them into this bad situation, and you shouldn't be the one getting them out of it, either. You could simply hand her everything you've found and walk away."

"I can't," Thuan said. "I have to see it through. That'd just be cowardice."

"Ah. Principles," Asmodeus said, in the tone of someone who had very few. "Van?" He stopped, shook his head. "No, that's unfair to ask you."

Van said, haltingly, "I just want him away from me.

I—" she closed her fists. "I want to be safe, and I want my family to be safe as well. I want to *live*."

"See?" Asmodeus's voice was curt. And, to Van, "There is absolutely no shame in doing whatever is necessary to survive. None. Do you understand?"

Van swallowed. "Sometimes there is more honour in death—" she started, and Asmodeus laughed.

"Hollowing yourself out for the sake of those who'd use your death for their own gain? No. That's just making it easier for them to win."

Van stared at him. "That's not—"

"What you've been taught?" Asmodeus came to stand by her, eyes staring into hers. "You have to understand the game is rigged. That if you play by the rules, there will always be someone to bend them to their advantage, or set them aside."

"Asmodeus—"

Asmodeus's voice was bleak. "Rules aren't going to help her, Thuan. Surely you must see that. Rules favour the established. That's Dang Quang."

Van said, finally, "Please. I'll do what it takes. Just keep me alive," and something painful shifted in Thuan's chest.

"Of course we will," Asmodeus said. His voice was matter of fact, but he hadn't broken eye contact with her.

Thuan started to say they could leave her with the delegation, and knew that wouldn't solve anything. Neither could they send half their guard home with her. He said, finally, "If we solve this, Hong Chi will be in our debt.

There's nothing Dang Quang will be able to raise against Van."

"If."

"Please," Thuan said. "Just a little longer. You may be able to live with the knowledge that your inaction brought wholesale destruction, but I can't."

A silence. Asmodeus was by his side again, tipping his head to look into his eyes, his fingers' warmth slowly spreading to Thuan's whole face. "Sentimental," he said, but his voice was softer. "And you're being unfair. If I bring wholesale destruction, it will most definitely be deliberate."

"Of course. How else?" Thuan smiled. It felt a little less forced than it had, earlier.

"Two days," Asmodeus said.

That wasn't a lot. Thuan opened his mouth to protest, and then saw Van's still-pale face when Asmodeus moved away. "Yes. Two days. And then you can march everyone, including me, back to Hawthorn, but you're the one who's going to have to come up with the diplomatic excuse."

"Oh, I have a store of them for such occasions, believe me." Asmodeus smiled. "Then it's agreed. Van?"

"My lord?"

"I asked you earlier whether you believed me when I said I would keep you from harm at all cost. Do you?" A pause, then, "You can say no, and we'll do this another way."

"I—" Van frowned. She said, finally, "I think you mean it."

"Good," Asmodeus said. "You'll stay with me, then."

"Asmodeus," Thuan said.

A look that could have shrivelled stone. "You think you're better placed to safeguard her?"

"That's not—"

"That's *exactly* the point," Asmodeus said. "And you know it."

"Fine, then. Have it your way."

"Good." Asmodeus didn't make any kind of witty comeback, which Thuan was grateful for. "Now where to?"

Thuan, exhausted from the argument and still not entirely sure he'd made the right decision, struggled to remember what had been going on. "Ministry of Personnel."

"I thought it was the Ministry of Rites?"

"The postings, yes," Thuan said. "The complete files are all going to be at the Ministry of Personnel, though, because they're the ones who keep track of the careers of officials. Did you hear back from Madeleine on that powder?"

"No," Asmodeus said. "But Van and I are going to go and ask her. And possibly go check out tailors, if we can. Does that meet with your approval?" His voice was low and mocking.

Thuan wasn't sure, anymore, of what he should be thinking or doing. "I guess it'll have to do. Let's go."

* * *

Thuan lost count of time at the Ministry of Personnel. It was perhaps not as vast a shambles as the Ministry of Rites, but it would be New Year's soon, and everyone was trying to finish up on their work as early as they could.

The Ministry was mostly underground, a vast network of caverns so deep no light penetrated. The rock walls had been scrubbed clean of algae and barnacles, and covered in a network of book alcoves from which what looked like an army of officials were withdrawing scrolls: people were so numerous and moving so much that even the usual shoals of fish of the citadel gave the place a wide berth. No one had time for anyone, and certainly not for an outsider like Thuan.

It would have been restful if he had any idea where to start: the smell of old paper and brine, and the magic of preservation spells, reminded him of the library; of quiet and happy times when he'd been able to withdraw from the world.

He missed that calm, that sense of hallowed purpose: that narrowness of the universe making sense.

Finally, a crab-official took pity on him. "Your Highness."

"I have... a particular problem, elder aunt," Thuan said. He'd considered what to say on the way there. Kim Diep knew that he was investigating, so it wasn't as though he'd be able to hide his inquiries from actual Harmony of Heaven members. What mattered was looking discreet enough that the official wouldn't think anything was amiss. And there, not being of the court would help—to some extent, he could rely on his current reputation as an eccentric outsider (he'd have sent Asmodeus for that, except that Asmodeus's formal Viet was limited, and that he'd certainly not have the patience to stand still for that long). "I went to pay my respects to my ancestors in the dynasty lineage temple. I gave some strings of cash to the official there, and I made a mistake and gave them a piece of jade that belonged to my mother mixed in with the cash. I went back to see if I could sort things out, but no one seems to have seen that official since." He shaped his face into a grimace. "I was distracted at having to manage my husband and I really shouldn't have made that mistake."

"Mmm." She was middle-aged with steel-grey hair, and pincers that expertly plucked the paper from his grasp. He'd redrawn Van's sketch with only the overall size, because a full body shape would have looked creepy. "That's going to be difficult. What gender were they?"

That was the part Thuan had been dreading. "It was dark," he said, plaintively. "I was hoping you maybe would have a list of people missing from the court of imperial sacrifices at the moment, with pictures? I'm sorry, my memory is really, really bad. All I know is that they were a dragon."

"Mmmm." As stories went, it was somewhere between indifferent and really transparently bad, but better than "we have a blood-soaked tunic and burnt bones". "Wait here," the official said.

He sat there, watching people withdraw rolls from alcove and take it to tables, where they'd animatedly talk, stabbing the paper with clawed hands. Dragons and crabs and fishes, the familiar background noise of the waves— if he closed his eyes, it was easy to remember the library, the way the doors would open and shut, the particular set of shelves he'd crouched by, devouring stories of earlier dynasties like lotus seeds and trying to forget the knot in his belly that the real-life intrigues circling around him like sharks would end him. He had that same knot now: both Kim Diep and Dang Quang—assuming they weren't working together—were adept at navigating the court in a way that he wasn't. His only assets were a resourceful thief who wasn't supposed to be his retainer, and a husband whose ideas of getting things done was finding someone to hurt. Neither Van nor Asmodeus would be able to sort out his particular tangle.

Hong Chi could. He'd find enough evidence for her, and she'd make sure that Van was safe. She'd come through. She always had. He forced himself to breathe slowly, evenly.

At length, the official came back with a list. "Here," she said. Thuan's heart sank, because it was *pages* long. "That's everyone who left the Ministry of Rites, whether on short or long-term leave, or because they resigned. No pictures, but you'll have date and place of birth."

"Thank you," Thuan said. "Are they all dragons?" He scanned down the list. The names were certainly suggestive of dragon families.

"I put a note next to those who weren't," the official said. A frown. "That particular Court is very... uniform."

A polite way to say that being a dragon was still the best way to get the good official postings in the civil service, and that as a crab she must have keenly felt that she was being passed over. "I know," Thuan said. "Thank you. I'll have a look." He debated giving her money, but he didn't want to contribute to what looked like enough corruption going around in the system. And, in any case, the currency she wanted likely wasn't that. Respect, then. "I'm very grateful, elder aunt."

"Hmmm." She looked at him, head cocked. "This is about something more than jade, isn't it?"

Thuan froze like a mouse caught in a cat's gaze. "Elder aunt."

She hadn't moved.

When caught in a lie, throw in just enough of the truth to be believable. "It... concerns my husband."

"Ah." Good, she'd heard of Asmodeus. Then again, news of him usually got around.

"I'm worried he may have done something improper, and I need to track that person down urgently."

"Ah." She stared at him for a while. His panic was genuine, and she had to see it. "I see. Well, whatever it is, I hope you can sort it out in time."

"Thank you. I'd... appreciate if you kept it to yourself," Thuan said. He thought she would: she looked decent enough. And if she didn't... well, Asmodeus's reputation would suffer, but it wasn't as if it could sink any lower in the kingdom anyway.

"Of course." She drew herself to her full height, which made her tower over him, pincers and all. "Ancestors watch over you, child."

Thuan reflected ruefully, as he left the ministry, that his ancestors must have been working overtime.

Thuan's mild sense of progress being made lasted only until he got back to their courtyard of the citadel—and found his way barred by two guards. "Your highness."

"Oh, let him through," an unfamiliar voice said.

Inside, it was chaos. The courtyard was overrun by guards and officials, and their quarters were barricaded. The smell of blood hung in the air so thick Thuan's stomach roiled. What had happened?

Asmodeus. Sharp, stabbing fear in his chest. Surely he wouldn't—

"Your highness." A forbidding looking official of the third rank with a topknot, and the glistening skin of a dolphin. "My name is Minh Linh. I'm captain of the palace guard," she said. "Where is your husband?"

Thuan looked down. On the threshold of their apartment was a body: Dang Quang's, the official who'd been so keen on Van. His heart sank. "I don't know," he said. "I spent the afternoon at the Ministry of Rites. I haven't seen him at all since then. Can I have a look?"

The guard watching over the body looked unhappy, but Minh Linh gestured. "Go ahead."

Thuan knelt. Dang Quang's face was frozen in a rictus. He'd been stabbed: a short, reflex thrust to the belly, followed by other shallower cuts on the chest—and a final one to the heart, with the knife that had done it planted all the way to the hilt. It was Asmodeus all over: the first cut had probably been self-defence, but the next few ones, the slow and shallow ones, had been to make the agony worse. And then the flourish at the end, when Asmodeus got bored or when Dang Quang slipped into shock.

Great. There was no way Thuan could pass this off as Dang Quang's fault, but he had to try. And where was Van? He assumed all of this had at least started to protect Van rather than on a whim—Asmodeus *was* angry and frustrated, but he was not that out of control.

"Do you have any witnesses?" he asked.

"Only from afar. They heard screams," Minh Linh said, curtly, as Thuan got up and brushed off silt from his trousers. "And an argument between the murdered official and your husband."

"Screams? His?"

"A woman's to start with." Minh Linh sighed. "Look, it's New Year's and I want to go home, your Highness. We know it was your husband, and right now his best outlook is to turn himself in. The courts will be lenient."

Or very harsh, to make it clear House Hawthorn didn't have the right to interfere in the dragon kingdom's affairs at all. "I don't think that's the case," Thuan said, sharply. "And I can't help you, I'm afraid. I don't know where he is."

Minh Linh cocked her head, watching him with beady eyes. Her teeth were small, triangular and unpleasantly sharp. "No, you don't, don't you? But you're still the person he's most likely to contact." She gestured towards the doors of his apartment. "You can stay inside, but right now you're not to wander elsewhere in the citadel."

"Wait—" Thuan said. "Wait—"

But she'd already wandered off, leaving him a prisoner in his own quarters.

It wasn't the first time Thuan had been under house arrest. He wasn't in danger personally this time: and it made it paradoxically worse, because he wasn't worrying on his own behalf, but on Asmodeus's and Van's.

He'd tried Van's tracking disk: what he'd got was a confused flurry of corridors somewhere in the imperial citadel, before Asmodeus's characteristically forceful magic had cut it off. So not only on the run but unsure whether they could trust him at all.

Great.

His nascent headache was not getting any better. On the plus side, they were both alive—wanted for the murder of an official but alive.

Not much comfort.

He couldn't blame them for wanting to remain out of

reach: all of this had happened because he'd insisted on staying. Because he thought that he could help Hong Chi. No, not help, do her work. Asmodeus was right: it hadn't been his prerogative in the first place, but now he couldn't just leave things unfinished.

He'd tried to reach Hong Chi, but the guards wouldn't take his messages, even to another official: Minh Linh must have convinced them he'd do anything to save his husband. And in the meantime whatever the society had killed for was inexorably hurtling towards its conclusion: a large and disruptive incident that would be enough to convince officials to openly rebel against a dynasty that had lost the Mandate of Heaven. Kim Diep, even if she'd had no part in this, must have been laughing at him.

He must have slept, at some point. Eaten food that he didn't remember putting in his mouth—some kind of noodle soup swiftly whisked away by the guard. Minh Linh came in and checked in on him, satisfied he'd gone nowhere. Thuan asked her about notifying someone, told her the dynasty was in danger: she got huffy and pointed out that the proper channels had been respected, which meant that the report on what he was doing was buried somewhere in paperwork somewhere in the Grand Secretariat, wending its way up to the Empress.

He tried Van's tracking disk again, got cut off again. This time the vibe was distinctly annoyed.

Great. Just great.

Well, if he was going to get bored, he might as well find something to keep busy. He grabbed the list he'd got from the Ministry of Rites, a spare paintbrush, and sat down to compare notes.

It was a long, long list, and he could very easily see why Grandmother had been grumbling: the entries were haphazard, and way too many people were leaving—he hoped they'd been replaced by new civil servants, but so many people leaving usually meant an exodus of the good ones. Insofar as wounds went, he was looking at a hemorrhage.

He removed everyone who wasn't of the fourth rank, everyone who wasn't a dragon, and everyone who didn't belong to the Court of Imperial Sacrifices. The list, unfortunately, was still large, because he couldn't be absolutely certain that the victim was actually physically involved with the worship of imperial ancestors, and the cult itself involved quite a bit of logistics beyond the temples.

The list was still sizeable. What had Van said? Shoulder spurs and not very wealthy. He couldn't check for spurs, but he looked over the brief career summaries. A lot of fourth-rank posts came with large money appointments or titles that provided strings of cash. He struck those off.

That left him with five names, all of them working at different locations in the imperial citadel. Rong Van An Nam, from the Palace Medical Service. Rong Thi Oanh Vu, from the Court Storehouses. Tran Thi Khanh Ngoc, from the Court of Seals. Pham Thi Thanh Tam, from the Office of the National Altars. Le Van Huong Thao, from the Imperial Music Office.

"Hum, my lord?"

Thuan raised his eyes. It was Madeleine, House Haw-thorn's alchemist, standing limned in the darkness of the door—outside, night had fallen in the usual way of the kingdom of the Seine, the sun plummeting into the water and abruptly stealing away the light. Was it evening already? He must have missed lunch.

"How did you get past the guards?"

"Oh," Madeleine wrung her hands. She was mid-dle-aged, with greying hair, and a perpetual air of worry that only seemed to taper off whenever Asmodeus was in the room. She was also carrying a leather shoulder bag with the arms of Hawthorn, which looked to be heavier than she was. "Véronique had to argue with them quite a bit, but they seemed satisfied we weren't going to break you out."

Thuan snorted. Three not always practically-minded scientists were definitely an unlikely rescue party, though of course appearances could be deceptive. "I hope you're all right?" he said. "You and the rest of the delegation."

"Oh. No, we're fine. It's only Lord Asmodeus they're worried about. They think we're barbaric and individu-alist and not much loyalty to superiors can be expected of us."

"It *is* an uncannily accurate description of most House politics," Thuan said. Including most of House Hawthorn's, unfortunately. "Did you see him before he disappeared?"

Madeleine grimaced. "Yes, he and the new

dependent—Van? He was headed back to your quarters to pick up something before going into the city to ask tailors."

Where instead, he'd met Dang Quang hell-bent on claiming Van back. "I see."

"Is he all right?"

Thuan shrugged. She was disastrous at politics: of course, even if he'd known, he wouldn't have told her. But she was in luck. If 'luck' was the proper name for a rather large-size helping of bad fortune. "I don't know where he is. But he's resourceful."

And he also had the entire imperial guard after him, which was less comforting.

Madeleine didn't look reassured. He couldn't blame her. "I take it you came here to report on the powder?"

"Yes," Madeleine said. She put a cotton bag on the table—Thuan suddenly saw she'd been wearing gloves. He'd been so busy worrying about Asmodeus he'd failed to notice.

"Bad, I take it. Wait. Asmodeus said it didn't do anything to food."

"No," Madeleine said. "That's because it mostly breaks down crystals."

Thuan raised an eyebrow. "You're going to need to unpack this a little more. Like jewelry?"

"Here," Madeleine said. She picked the bowl of water on the reception room's table, and shook some of the powder in it, grimacing. Then she put a small ring in it. Bubbles rose to the surface, along with a familiar flash of magic. She withdrew large tongs from her shoulder bag, and used them to fish out the ring, holding it out so Thuan could see. The stone in it looked oddly wrong, its facets slightly out of alignment—something about the way the light struck it…

Madeleine shook it, and it just came apart, disintegrating into fine, sandy powder. "Crystals are a lattice," she said. "If you can weaken the bonds in the proper way…"

"Hmm," Thuan said. "I can see that, but we don't really have a lot of these rings in the imperial city."

Wait.

He went back to the list of people who might be the missing official. There. Tran Thi Khanh Ngoc, an official in the Court of Seals. "Madeleine—"

"Mm?" Madeleine was shaking the tongs in water, trying to get the powder from them.

"Is jade a crystal?"

"Of course. Jadeite or nephrite, depending on the characteristics and the value—it will alter them too, except perhaps with larger cracks…" She stopped, then. "You don't care."

"I do care very much," Thuan said. The regnal seals. The packed collection of jade and silver seals used by the Empress to sign everything from promotions to national decrees, to answers to memorials. The beating heart, not only of the civil service, but of the entire empire. "Do you know what Phat Thuc is?"

Madeleine looked panicked. "My lord?"

"It's a cleaning ceremony," Thuan said. "In the last

month of the year, on the twentieth day, all the empress' seals are taken from the cabinets where they're stored and put into a bath of water with scented flowers, and then dried with red cloth before being stored for the New Year's period. It means that the civil service and the dynasty are resting. And on New Year's Day the cabinets will be opened, and the seals unveiled again."

And what would happen, if they crumbled into dust as they were being put away into the cabinet, in full view of the most senior officials of the court?

Think think think. "What day are we?"

"My lord?"

But he knew, didn't he? The lunar calendar took some thought to align to most days, but the last month was easy, because all he had to do was countdown to New Year's Eve. It was the evening of the nineteenth day of the twelfth month. They had one night left, barely: the cabinets would be open at dawn, the water lovingly cleansed by dragons and scented with the flowers the petals of which Asmodeus had found—and the seals would crack and crumble into dust, and the society would have its unsubtle, incontrovertible message: that the dynasty had lost the Mandate of Heaven, for what kind of Empress could still claim to rule, with no seals to pass on her orders?

Thuan hesitated. He hated playing the game of politics. He hated the court and the faction and everything it stood for. But Asmodeus was right: he'd been miserable at court, but it didn't change who he was and the power he wielded—and what he chose to be responsible for, in the end. "I want you to do something for me," he said to Madeleine.

She looked at him, eyes wide. "My lord."

"You're going to need Véronique's help. Go see the Empress Dowager, and tell her you're coming from the bookish one, not the ruthless one." He fingered his own personal seal, the one he wasn't supposed to give to anyone for anything. He couldn't give it to her, because they'd search her when she came out, foreigner or not. "How good is your memory?"

Madeleine started. "I don't know—"

"Me neither." Thuan walked to the table, and pressed his own seal into vermillion paste, and then into paper. "If you can reproduce this, it should help you past the eunuchs."

"The bookish one. I don't understand…"

"You don't," Thuan said. "But she will."

Madeleine stared, for a while, at the imprint of the seal. "I'm not too sure I can memorise it."

Thuan shrugged, with a lightness he didn't feel. "Of course not. Do your best. Thank you."

He waited with bated breath when she got out—he heard her say something to the guard, and then Véronique sharply pointing out something—and then silence, and he couldn't even be sure what had happened.

It was a lousy, lousy plan. This late at night, the Dowager probably wouldn't want to receive anyone, let alone a foreigner like Madeleine. She liked Asmodeus, but in a way that an adult liked children: she was fond of him but certainly wouldn't want to swing her considerable weight on his behalf—and maybe not even on behalf of Thuan. But she was still way, way easier to reach than Second Aunt.

He could only wait, and hope—and pray that it was, in the end, all going to be enough.

Thuan did try to convince the guards he needed to see Minh Linh, and that it was urgent. He hadn't expected much from this, and it didn't work: the guards laughed and said he was raving, and turned away from him. Maybe he'd see Minh Linh at some point, but he had no doubt she'd tell him the same thing again, that proper protocol was being followed.

Thuan must have slept: he woke up with a start. The room was suffused with the grey light before dawn, a prelude to a sunrise that would come as fast and as sudden as the sunset had, flooding the room with the dappled light of underwater shallows. Almost time, and he had failed.

You're not the one who got them into this bad situation, and you shouldn't be the one getting them out of it, either.

I have to see it through.

He'd failed. Arrogance and unwillingness to face the truth that Asmodeus had seen: that this was all larger than him and that the world wasn't going to fold itself to accommodate him. That Hong Chi should have had much better ideas than giving something this sensitive to the family outsider, the prince who had married away because no one had really cared about where he went.

But with that ice-water awareness came another one: every idea, no matter how doomed it might seem, was worth a try.

He closed his eyes as if he were meditating, and sought out Van's tracking disk again—got, for the briefest of moments, a vision of rock spurs in the gardens, felt Asmodeus's magic grab him, ready to squeeze the connection out of existence—and in that one suspended moment he sent through an image of the regnal seals fractured and falling into dust, and the words "Phat Thuc"—and felt Van's shock of recognition, as she instinctively grabbed Asmodeus's hand to prevent him from cutting Thuan off—and then her panic as she realised she'd set herself against him—but Asmodeus simply closed his fingers on hers, and shook his head, his face hardening, his mouth opening on words Thuan didn't need to hear to make out.

Too risky. Not getting involved. And something rather sharper and angrier that Thuan couldn't quite make out, about danger to Van if they got arrested.

It cut off with the finality of an executioner's garrotte, leaving Thuan shaking on his bed.

They weren't going to help; but then why had he thought they ever would? Asmodeus had made his position very clear, and why would Van risk her own freedom and life to save the dynasty, when one of its own celebrated officials had been the one to break her life and hound her?

It wasn't fair; and perhaps it had never been.

Outside, the bi-hour of the cat rang, and the greyness of the sky was getting washed out. Not long before the ceremony now. Not long before it was too late.

Thuan got up, ready to harangue the guards once more to let him out—but the door opened before he got a chance.

What?

It was a eunuch wearing blue robes—his face was vaguely familiar, and then Thuan realised it was the one who'd accompanied him to Grandmother's apartments. He bowed and gestured, wordlessly, towards the door.

Thuan walked towards it, to find the guards gone, and the courtyard emptied of every single retainer. Everything was curiously silent and still. He looked up: the sky was gray, the light streaked with pink and trembling on the verge of sunrise.

"Your grandmother requests your presence," the eunuch said.

Thuan shook his head. "There's no time. The regnal seals, where are they kept?"

"The Palace of Audiences, your Highness. But—"

The eunuch opened his mouth to say something more, about filial piety and the duty owed to elders.

"There's no time," Thuan said. "Tell Grandmother—or better yet, Hong Chi—they're going to destroy the seals."

"Your Highness!"

Thuan didn't bother to wait, but started running—and then shifting into full dragon shape, flying through the pillars of the courtyard and praying very very hard he wouldn't knock over any of them while still struggling to adapt to his much larger size.

In dragon shape, the pillared corridors between the various palace buildings were much harder to navigate: Thuan, swinging wildly, narrowly missed hitting a pillar or an official or both. People scattered, throwing him dark looks. He could imagine the flood of memorials complaining about the failure of the imperial prince to conform to propriety—he was going to have *so* many explanations to give, and so many of them unpleasant, too. He flew over the wide expanse of the gardens, over a large labyrinth of pebbles—over the Imperial Theatre and the faint sound of zithers and drums from the musicians practising, the dynastic urns, the residences of the various princesses...

He'd not done this for two years—more, because he'd seldom actually been *flying* through the citadel. The Palace of Audiences was on the edge of the Purple Forbidden City nearest the main gate: a place for the Empress to work and receive officials, not for her private life or for her harem. It should have been quite close to where Thuan and Asmodeus had been lodged, but he'd got lost somewhere, and the sun was rising over the roofs of the citadel, gilding the longevity tiles and throwing dappled reflections over the algae and mould and cracks.

Come on come on come on.

There.

Another corridor and another garden, and he'd be in the right place—he could hear the zithers accompanying the return procession of officials, with the water from the well at the centre of the city, and he only had to fly a little further—

Something hard and unshakeable rose out of nowhere, and he hit it head-on. He fell on the floor, everything spinning and wobbling; tried to rise again, found himself entangled in the meshes of a net of *khi*-water—tightening with every attempt he made at freeing himself.

What—what had happened? No. No.

Footsteps, low and measured. "Ah, child." Kim Diep's voice was regretful. "I did warn you. Told you to go home."

"This is my home," Thuan said, twisting to try and throw the net off, but it didn't work. His claws kept sliding off the net. Think. *Khi*-water. He needed to be using magic, but he kept convulsing.

Laughter that wasn't so much gloating as wistful. Someone was pushing him and the net away: all he could see was glimpses of the floor, and then stunted, dry algae. The music was receding. Someone asked Kim Diep a question that was so fast and so accented Thuan didn't hear it.

She said, "Just keep him away from the Palace of Audiences. There's no need for bloodshed."

"There *will* be bloodshed!" He tried to weave *khi*-water,

and it kept sliding off just like his claws had. What had they used for the net? "Do you really think this is going to be a friendly discussion and a handing off of power to a new dynasty?"

"Oh, I meant specifically your blood," Kim Diep said. She knelt by his side, head cocked—he could barely see her because of the net, but her eyes shone in the darkness. "You're a hindrance and impossibly annoying, but I like you. Never giving up."

Thuan wasn't feeling like giving up, but he was running out of options. The net was tight around his whole body now, a chokehold holding him with spine curved and head sunk between his own scales, and his limbs flat against his body. It wasn't uncomfortable, but equally he couldn't move. He was on tiles now, in what sounded like a suspiciously deserted part of the citadel—which meant the society had cleared it. This close to the Palace of Audiences, there wouldn't be a deserted area in sight. What time was it now? The light wasn't grey or pink anymore, and the music had stopped. The officials would be back at the palace, opening the cabinet and revealing row after row of seals, about to plunge them into poisoned water...

He tried shifting back to his human shape, which was much smaller—and the net followed him, shrinking so fast he didn't even have time to start untangling himself. So not only was he stuck inside, but now he didn't have claws or fangs anymore.

Not good.

Think think think. He couldn't appeal to her goodness. But perhaps he could play on her fears. "It's still going to take time," he said, twisting against the net with the forlorn hope it would work.

"Oh, I'd say the citadel is a powder keg ready to blow."

Thuan grimaced. "I've spent too much time in the library. Dynasties don't fall in one fell swoop. Order doesn't just vanish. Even if all the regnal seals disintegrate, even if someone in a province rises up tomorrow—even if they're an official in this city, in this citadel, order will prevail. If only for a time. And in that time, they're going to make arresting and condemning you a priority."

Please please, ancestors.

Laughter from Kim Diep. "So you're suggesting I should stop now so they can arrest me better?" A frown. "Or alternatively, you're making a very good case for me to simply kill you."

And burn the bones, the way they'd done with Khanh Ngoc's in the garden? "No," Thuan said, sharply. "I'm sure I'm not the only witness."

A shrug. "Leaving the six chambers isn't a crime anymore, and gently suggesting an area of the palace needs to be deserted is a mild disturbance of the peace."

"My point," Thuan said, choking on silt. "Please, elder aunt. If you stop this now we can still both pretend it never happened."

Kim Diep looked at him, for a while. "You mean it, don't you?" A sigh.

Thuan said, "I'll go to Grandmother or Second Aunt and ask them to set you free. You know I would."

"Yes." Kim Diep shifted, her feet crunching on dried algae. "I do."

"Please, elder aunt."

For a moment he thought he'd reached her; that he'd made her see—but then she shook her head. "Ah, child. I don't know how you could remain so naive about the way the world works."

"I'm not naive," Thuan said, stubbornly. "Things *can* change from the inside." Hawthorn had.

"Perhaps." Kim Diep's voice was sharp. "If there's a will to change. If priorities are made." A gentle snort. "If if if. Consider this, then: it shouldn't take a prince of imperial blood and a special favour for me to get what I want." She rose, and the net tightened around Thuan once more, drawing him huddled into himself. "Goodbye, dragon prince. With any luck you should be able to make it back to Hawthorn."

It was too late. He'd lost because he'd been too stubborn, too opinionated, too blind. Her footsteps receded away from him, and there was nothing but the shadow of his own body, the misery of the net's mesh holding him tight, the sense of his own failure.

He—

Other quiet, determined footsteps, and a flare of familiar magic.

"I don't think so," a cool voice said. "I do have strong objections to people roughing up my husband."

Kim Diep's footsteps had stopped—a clink of spears and knives, Asmodeus's gentle laughter. "I gave you your one single warning to keep out of my way."

And then a tumult of metal on metal, footsteps ringing, people screaming—Thuan trying to stretch once more, the net stubbornly refusing to give way. "Asmodeus!" he shouted. "Go warn them. I'll be fine."

A grunt, the soft sound of a knife sliding into flesh, and a body hitting the ground.

"You're demonstrably not fine," Asmodeus said, kneeling by his side and laying a hand on Thuan's skin through the mesh. The net loosened but didn't break: Van had cut into it with a blood-stained dagger drawn from her belt. She was shaking like a leaf.

"You're wasting time," Thuan said, to Asmodeus, who had started helping Van with taking the net apart. His fingers were releasing bursts of Fallen magic that contracted the mesh around Thuan's skin, a warm and not wholly unpleasant feeling that went all the way to Thuan's spine, a split second before these parts of the mesh dissolved into nothingness. It was painstaking and slow—link by link, patch by patch—and it wasn't going to be over in any good time.

"I'm seeing to my own." Asmodeus's voice was low and angry. "We've already had this discussion."

Thuan said—because he didn't know what else to say—"Please. You said I didn't respect your way of doing things, and I have no right to ask you to put yourself in danger."

"No, you don't."

"And I'm not asking Van because it would be unfair, and cowardly." The net loosened enough for Thuan to start unfolding his head, wincing as cramped muscles finally eased. He was in an empty room he couldn't identify, with an open door leading outside: the light was warm and still pink, the sun barely risen. Behind Van were scattered bodies in various states from wounded to unconscious to dying—Kim Diep was on her back with a dagger pinning her shoulder to the floor, eyes closed and entire body limp. The net still held more than half of him: his legs were bunched together in a way that made walking or flight impossible.

"My lord—" Van started.

"You said you wanted to live. You're scared, and you're the one who's got the most to lose," Thuan said.

"In that, if nothing else, he's entirely right." Asmodeus's face looked a fraction softer, which didn't change much. "He can't order you to do this, and he shouldn't."

"Please, Asmodeus. I'm just asking you to stand by me," Thuan said. He tried to slip free of the net, but his chest and lower half were still encased in what felt like an unbreakable hold of *khi*-water. "Because it's important to me, and it's going to take way too much time to get me free."

"Emotional blackmail?"

"No," Thuan said. "Because blackmail is when you don't have a choice. You do."

"So you'll forgive me if I just free you and we walk

away from this, instead of warning the Empress or who-ever it is I should be risking my neck for?" Asmodeus's voice was sharp. He laid a hand on the net on Thuan's chest, and Fallen magic contracted it until Thuan's breath was a diffuse, throbbing fire in his lungs. "Don't lie, Thuan."

"Asmodeus." Thuan closed his eyes, for a brief moment. The net was tight and unbearably warm on his skin. Asmodeus was right: it was unfair, and too much to ask. "Fine. Just get me out of this and I'll go. It's my responsibility, not yours."

"And perhaps I don't want you to risk your life."

"That's my decision to make, not yours."

Asmodeus watched him, for a while, head cocked. Then he laughed. "Ah, dragon prince. You give up too easily," he said. He bent and kissed Thuan—a short, sharp thing that made the burning in Thuan's chest incoherent and needful—and rose. "You're most definitely getting me out of trouble afterwards." And, to Van, "What do I tell them?"

Van said something that Thuan didn't hear, because Asmodeus was stretching, and the ghost of great dark wings spread behind him with a noise like ten thousand banners unfurling—and then he started running towards the exit of the room, moving with the easy, sinuous ele-gance and speed of a large cat catching up with prey. Thuan watched him with his heart in his throat.

Ancestors, please let it not be too late. Please let it not be too late.

He barely heard the distant shouts—Asmodeus's voice raised in pitch-perfect Viet, followed by more forceful French, then the distant argument. And then, like an answer to his prayer, the music starting again, and Van's hand on his shoulder as, finally freed from the net, he made his way out of the room they'd shut him in, passing by unconscious and wounded officials; watched the procession of officials exit the Palace of Audiences carrying a water bowl as though it might bite—and only peaceful silence spreading over the citadel.

Then, and only then, did he allow himself to relax.

It was not over, of course. When Thuan finally walked into the Palace of Audiences with Van by his side, he found Asmodeus held in a ring of spears by guards, the Empress gone, and officials wanting explanations. This was followed, in quick order, by the eunuch from Grandmother who'd let Thuan out of his house arrest—who took one look at the situation and started ordering officials about in an authoritative manner eerily reminiscent of his mistress.

Asmodeus let himself be led off by the guards, with a significant glance at Thuan that he was being patient for Thuan's sake but that Thuan had better deliver on his end of the bargain soon, or sharp and stabby things were going to come out again.

Thuan and Van were sent back to their quarters to await an imperial audience, and Thuan sent Van—who was still shaking—to the reception room to get a tea and some food in her. He sat on the bed and mentally started rehearsing arguments for said audience, though he mainly counted on Hong Chi being there.

"My lord?"

He raised his head, and saw Van leaning in the door-frame with a cup of tea in her hands. "You look better," he said. "I don't know how you are feeling."

Van shrugged. She came into the bedroom, and laid the tea on the table, very deliberately and carefully. "I'm all right. Thank you."

"Thank *you*," Thuan said. "For freeing me. And I'm sorry. It must have been a shock. With Dang Quang."

Van grimaced. "I stabbed him. Well, the first time." Her face was still frozen in that odd expression between fear and elation. "He grabbed me in the courtyard, saying he wasn't letting go so easily, and I didn't know what else to do, and there was no way I was ever going back in his power…"

And Asmodeus had taken over. "I wouldn't worry about it," Thuan said. "They're going to owe us quite a few favours for this, and they'll smooth a lot of things out. Including that one."

"I guess so." Van stared at the tea, for a while. "He's all right," she said. "Your husband."

Ah, dragon prince. You give up too easily. Thuan rubbed his lips, feeling the warmth of Asmodeus's touch on them. "I'm not too sure these are the words I'd use."

Van said, finally, "I'd like to ask a favour."

Thuan said nothing, only waited.

"I want to go home," Van said. "To my town."

Thuan, startled, stared at her. Her fists were clenched, shifting into pincers. She must have expected him to say no. "You want to leave the House?"

"Asmodeus said—" Van closed her eyes. "He—was rigged. That I couldn't afford to play by the rules."

"He says lots of things. They're not always true."

"But these are." Van's voice was soft. "And they shouldn't be." She drew herself to her full height, and Thuan suddenly understood, seeing the closed pincers and the shimmering carapace, how formidable crabs could be. "I want to change it."

A silence. Thuan said, finally, "Are you doing this because you stood aside?" Because she'd freed Thuan instead of running to the Empress; of risking her own life to warn them.

"Yes," Van said. "And don't tell me it's not a reason."

Thuan said nothing, for a while. At length, "We've been making too many decisions for you as it is, so no, I'm not going to tell you anything. If being amnestied and going back is what you want, then that's the way it's going to be. Or the way I'm going to try and make it be." He said, finally, "You don't sound very worried about Asmodeus."

Van was silent for a while. "No," she said. "I realised that…" she bit her lips. "I realised that, as scary as he was, there were scarier things."

And wouldn't that be a blow to Asmodeus's pride. But then again he must have known all of Van's worst fears: he had an uncanny instinct for these, a predator's scenting prey—just as he knew all of Thuan's worst fears: abandonment, loss—and, ultimately, turning away so much from what was right that he wouldn't dare look at himself in the mirror in the morning.

These things are true. And they shouldn't be.

Thuan stared at the table, pondering on righteousness, and rituals, and benevolence—and finally sat down, to draft a letter.

The imperial audience took place in the Empress's private office, not in the throne room, which didn't spare Thuan from having to make his way there *through* the throne room, between two aligned groups of officials, as if he were going up the aisles of a Catholic church. He'd sent off his letter the previous evening, signing it with his personal seal, and dressed that morning as if he were going into battle—finally choosing the red and gold robes of a prince rather than the swallowtail suit that would remind Second Aunt too much of the House. Van was trailing behind him, the marks on her arms hidden beneath the large, opaque sleeves of her robes.

The office was a simple room, the wooden carvings on the wall sparse, the desk a simple affair of red lacquered wood, and a few cupboards holding writing materials:

brushes, ink stones and rolls of paper. Second Aunt sat behind the desk reading a report: she was a middle-aged, forbidding dragon woman, wearing the yellow embroidered robes of her rank—but not her crown, though she didn't need to, in private. Hong Chi was by her side in full court robes—and Asmodeus was sitting in a chair, surrounded by guards. He had chains around his wrists and a very familiar expression on his face of patient indulgence wound very, very tight.

Thuan bowed, very low—because disrespecting propriety was not going to get him anywhere, and then asked, "The society?"

Hong Chi's face was expressionless. "We'll deal with them."

She grimaced, but it was Second Aunt who spoke. "That was a rather large disturbance."

"You hired us," Asmodeus said, rather drily. "You did know what you were getting into."

"*I* did not," Second Aunt said, mildly.

Ah. That was the problem, then. He'd suspected as much. Thuan threw a glance at Hong Chi, but she didn't appear to be moving. Too much in trouble of her own?

Asmodeus's face was creased in a broad, ironic smile. *Your cousin is playing you like a fiddle, and not a particularly good one at that.*

Thuan hesitated, then said, coldly, "I'm not playing games. Either Hong Chi has your confidence, or she doesn't." It was a deuced awkward position to be lecturing one's empress and elder, a very fine line to walk. "And why is Asmodeus still a prisoner?"

Hong Chi's voice was cool. "Because he stabbed an official in the palace."

Thuan opened his mouth to say he hadn't, and then realised that would be throwing Van to the tigers. Asmodeus got there first. "Your official was looking for trouble. Interfering with my personal business."

"That's not a reason—"

Asmodeus's voice was cool. "Trying to seize one of my dependents to torture her is, I think, a clear breach of House Hawthorn's diplomatic immunity."

"You have no diplomatic immunity." Second Aunt's voice was cold. "You're here as my relative, and that makes you subject to the law, same as anyone."

A shrug. "I see. Complaining about the broken plates on the way to the banquet. That's rather rich of you." He looked, thoughtfully, at the chains, and Fallen magic started glowing under his skin.

Thuan tried to find words, couldn't. It was all rather going downhill rather quickly.

Behind him, the door opened, and the wind carried in a hint of orchid perfume, and that particular smell of sandalwood and cedar. Second Aunt got up, hastily bowing, and Thuan did the same—even Asmodeus moved in a clink of chains, his head briefly dipping down.

"Grandmother."

The Empress Dowager's gaze raked the participants in the meeting. "I see I'm just in time." She sat down in the chair right next to Asmodeus, and gestured to the eunuch who had accompanied her. "Well, off you go. Free him."

Second Aunt opened her mouth, closed it. Asmodeus's face was a study in carefully disguised shock: he looked to Thuan, who merely nodded grimly. *Not playing by the rules.* Or rather, creatively selecting the bits he was going to uphold. He couldn't order Second Aunt about, but her own mother could—if appraised of the meeting and its stakes for Thuan and Asmodeus by a letter from her grandson, for instance.

The chains fell off. Asmodeus stretched—rather too theatrically—and then laid his elbow on the arm of the chair, and rested his chin on his hand, looking at the entire scene with the clear expression of someone waiting, glass of wine in hand, for the entertaining fireworks to start. He was silent, but he probably wasn't going to remain so for long.

"You should be ashamed." Grandmother's voice was cold.

"I don't see what you mean," Second Aunt said. "I'm upholding the order of Heaven. as is proper."

"Hmmmf." Grandmother snorted. "I told Asmodeus already that the kingdom has gotten weak."

"And your solution is *foreigners* running amok in the citadel stabbing officials?"

Ah. There was the rub, then. Not Hong Chi's decision to give this investigation to outsiders, but the diplomatic tangle of involving House Hawthorn to interfere in Second Aunt's own running of the citadel.

Grandmother picked up the cup of tea the eunuch had mysteriously summoned for her, and sipped at it, rheumy eyes thoughtful. "No. My solution is executing everyone who so much looks as if they're thinking of disloyalty."

Hong Chi winced. Asmodeus's smile was even broader. Second Aunt spluttered, and then said, "That's not the way things go nowadays, Mother."

"The way things go nowadays is you have a secret society getting close enough to the regnal seals to create an uproar. Not to mention imprisoning my own grandson a few paces away from the Palace of Audiences."

That would be Thuan—who was still busy putting his arguments together. He'd hoped to offer Van; to send her to some high post in the civil service, so she could push change through—the letter to Grandmother, obviously, had only aimed to get Asmodeus free. But if the problem was outsiders, his offering a former House Hawthorn dependent—never mind one with a particular history— was not going to solve anything.

Be honest: it had never looked likely to solve anything.

These things are true. And they shouldn't be.

Consider this, then: it shouldn't take a prince of imperial blood and a special favour for me to get what I want.

Thuan said, "You have a choice. You can purge every discontent in blood, knowing it will touch more than the society. Or—" he took a deep breath, aghast at his own audacity—"You can push change through."

A short, sharp intake of breath from Van; a look that could have frozen stone from Grandmother. Before

Second Aunt could protest, Thuan said, "You're trying not to make waves. You want to keep your officials contented and your throne safe. And it's those same officials that are causing harm and spreading discontent. The cost of not making waves is that, further away from the citadel, people choke under misrule. If you want to change things, these officials have to go. They have to receive the punishment for corruption; for murder; for closing their eyes to the misery of their own people."

"You don't understand politics." Second Aunt's voice was cold.

Asmodeus said, "I agree. He's always been far too idealistic." A shrug. "Personally, I'd go for the first option."

Hong Chi said, "We need time." She sounded raw and desperate, repeating an argument she must have made too many times.

"You're out of time," Thuan said, gently. "Look at the society. It's got tendrils in the citadel. That's how far discontent goes."

Second Aunt looked at Thuan. "So you're telling me what to do."

Thuan stared at her. "Are you going to tell me I'm a foreigner too and this isn't my home?"

A snort. "Don't be silly. You're my nephew."

"I don't live in the kingdom anymore, but it's a place that still matters to me. I care," Thuan said, softly, desperately, and he didn't know if he was speaking to Hong Chi or to her. "I'm just telling you the options you have. Pick something. Anything."

Grandmother said, "I'm with Asmodeus. Kill them all. Or the first few, at any rate. That should make the next ones less bold."

"I'm going to run out of people to kill if everyone is unsatisfied," Second Aunt said, drily. She was looking at Thuan. "And I suppose you'll be telling me not to make an example of Kim Diep, next?"

Thuan shrugged. "I'm not making suggestions for the entirety of dragon kingdom politics." He sought other words, found only a gaping hole, and the only truth that he could hold. "I just want to make sure we do the right thing."

Asmodeus's face was a study in... Thuan would have said sarcasm, but actually the expression looked a great deal like fondness.

"The right thing." Hong Chi's voice was flat.

Thuan said, quoting the First Teacher, "Lead through moral force, not by means of rules and punishments." He felt as exhausted as if he'd just run a marathon.

Second Aunt watched him, for a while. "The bookish one," she said.

"Sometimes books are what we need."

A sigh, from her. "There will be a heavy price to pay for this."

"There is always the first solution," Grandmother said.

"Oh, I haven't forgotten," Second Aunt said. Her smile was wide, and the stuff of Thuan's nightmares. "The society will need to be purged, and you sound like you're bored in your palace, Mother. Your agents can help Hong Chi track them down." And, to Thuan, "Was that all?"

Thuan looked at Van—who hadn't moved or spoken. He smiled, with a brightness he no longer felt. "Actually, not quite."

Later—much, much later, when everything had blurred into far too much talking and posturing, Asmodeus walked Thuan back to their quarters in uncanny silence. He remained silent while Thuan brewed tea for them both, grassy and light for himself, sharper for Asmodeus, who liked his bitter and on the overbrewed side. Asmodeus took the cup from Thuan's hand, and leant against the wall, watching as Thuan sat down on the bed, feeling as though nothing held him upright anymore.

Thuan said, finally, "I think Van will be all right." Second Aunt had barely balked when he'd mentioned amnesty, but then again she'd had to swallow a much bitterer pill. They'd left Van the House Hawthorn tracking disk: all the formalities of reinstating her could wait until the following day.

"Oh, I have no doubt," Asmodeus said. He sipped at his tea. "She's smart and resourceful, and her new post should come with a significant salary. Your cousin said she wanted Van to be part of the new crop of imperial censors, going out to arrest the corrupt officials. I have no doubt she'll take to it as a fish—sorry, a crab—to water."

A silence. He was watching Thuan with an expression

Thuan couldn't quite parse. Thuan felt winded and uncertain, and with a cold emptiness in his stomach that he wasn't quite sure was shame or fear, or both.

Thuan said, finally, "I'm sorry."

A raised eyebrow. "You did get me out of trouble. And with such panache. It's almost unlike you."

"You know what I mean." Thuan exhaled. "I shouldn't have insisted on seeing this through. You were already indulging me by coming down here, and I dragged you into politics and into risking your own life. And you lost Van, too, which I know makes you unhappy. You hate letting go of dependents, and I made that decision on your behalf."

A creak, on the bed: Asmodeus, sitting by his side, the tea cup casually left on the bedside table. "Actually, running through the citadel while trying to evade the guard was a much better thrill than having to sit through endless banquets with your family. And Dang Quang deserved all of what he got." A smile. "And yes, we lost Van, but I get to help your grandmother deal with the Harmony of Heaven society. I'm a little bit disappointed Van didn't take me up on my offer to visit retribution on Kim Diep. She was, after all, the one who tried to foist Van on us as a bribe, fully expecting Van to get tortured to death. Ah well. I should imagine punishment is coming to Kim Diep, one way or another."

"Asmodeus—" Thuan closed his eyes. "If you want, we can go home. I think you've given enough to the kingdom."

A touch of magic on his lips, stilling them, and other ones, pinning his arms by his side, as Asmodeus leant, his grey-green eyes transfixing Thuan—a finger drawing a slow circle on his lips. Something warm and unbearable rose within Thuan: he struggled to speak, but Asmodeus's magic held him fast. "Sssh, dragon prince. I said you should respect the way I live. That does go both ways." His fingers undid the fastening of Thuan's robes, slipping them down until Thuan sat in the midst of a sea of embroidered silk, dragons spreading around him—Asmodeus's hands rested, lightly, on Thuan's chest. Warmth spread out, magnetic and urgent, as his fingers gently drew the same circles on Thuan's skin, going upwards to the throat and Thuan's madly beating larynx. "Consider yourself forgiven. As for leaving—why would I? I have all I want here."

"Please," Thuan said, and the magic lifted enough that he could croak the word through a throat that felt aflame.

Laughter, good-humored and sharp, and then a push that sent Thuan sprawling on the bed, and Asmodeus moving to straddle him, pale skin glowing with magic. His spell brushed Thuan's neck and earlobes and lips, gently, slowly, back and forth until there was nothing left but moans in Thuan's throat.

Please please please.

"Ah, dragon prince. Yes, of course. Always and always." And Asmodeus bent over him, and the warmth of his body became Thuan's entire world.

Acknowledgements

Books are always a bit of an adventure, and I would like to thank the following people for reading this: Zoe Johnson, D Franklin, Likhain, Lynn E. O'Connacht, Alicia Fourie, Yan Baltazar, Juliet Kemp, and Fran Wilde. I would also like to thank my friends for their never-ending support during the writing and publishing of this: Samit Basu, Elizabeth Bear and Scott Lynch, Liz Bourke, Stephanie Burgis, Zen Cho, Vida Cruz, Kate Elliott, Stella Evans, Stevie Finegan, Alessa Hinlo, Inkantadora, Inksea, Vic James, Ghislaine Lai, Hana Lee, Ken Liu, Likhain and her partner, Rachel Monte, Laura J Mixon, Sarah Mueller, Emma Newman, Jeannette Ng, Natasha Ngan and Fab, Nina Niskanen, Nene Ornes, Sheila Perry, Victor R Fernando Ocampo, Cindy Pon, Gareth L Powell, Justina Robson, Tricia Sullivan and Tade Thompson.

Many thanks to Patrick Disselhorst, Lisa Rodgers and Joshua Bilmes for putting this book together; to Ravven for the cover art; to Juliet Kemp for the proofreading, and to John Berlyne for coordinating everything.

And finally, to my family, my parents and my sister and my children: thank you for being my rock.

About the Author

Aliette de Bodard lives and works in Paris, where she has a day job as a System Architect. She studied Computer Science and Applied Mathematics, but moonlights as a writer of speculative fiction. Aliette has won three Nebula Awards, a Locus Award, a British Fantasy Award and four British Science Fiction Association Awards, and was a double Hugo finalist (Best Series and Best Novella).

Most recently she published *The House of Sundering Flames* (Gollancz/JABberwocky Literary Agency, Inc.), the conclusion to her Dominion of the Fallen trilogy, set in a turn-of-the-century Paris devastated by a magical war–which also comprises *The House of Shattered Wings* (Roc/Gollancz, 2015 British Science Fiction Association Award, Locus Award finalist), and *The House of Binding Thorns* (Ace/Gollancz, 2017 European Science Fiction Society Achievement Award, Locus award finalist).

Her short story collection *Of Wars, and Memories, and Starlight* is out from Subterranean Press.

She is also the author of *The Tea Master and the*

Detective (2018 Nebula Award winner, 2018 British Fantasy Award winner, 2019 Hugo Award finalist), a murder mystery set on a space station in a Vietnamese Galactic empire, inspired by the characters of Sherlock Holmes and Dr. Watson; and *In the Vanishers' Palace*, a dark Beauty and the Beast retelling, where they are both women and the Beast is a dragon.

Visit her website www.aliettedebodard.com for free fiction (including further short stories set in the same universe as this one), Vietnamese and French recipes and more.

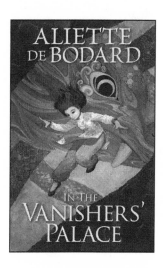

IN THE VANISHERS' PALACE

*In a ruined, devastated world, where the earth is poisoned and
beings of nightmares roam the land...*

*A woman, betrayed, terrified, sold into indenture to pay her
village's debts and struggling to survive in a spirit world.*

*A dragon, among the last of her kind, cold and aloof but desper-
ately trying to make a difference.*

When failed scholar Yên is sold to Vu Côn, one of the last dragons
walking the earth, she expects to be tortured or killed for Vu Côn's
amusement.

But Vu Côn, it turns out, has a use for Yên: she needs a scholar to tutor
her two unruly children. She takes Yên back to her home, a vast, vertig-
inous palace-prison where every door can lead to death. Vu Côn seems
stern and unbending, but as the days pass Yên comes to see her kinder
and caring side. She finds herself dangerously attracted to the dragon
who is her master and jailer. In the end, Yên will have to decide where
her own happiness lies—and whether it will survive the revelation of Vu
Côn's dark, unspeakable secrets...

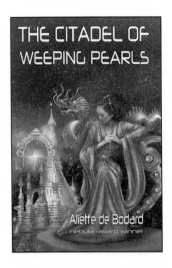

THE CITADEL OF WEEPING PEARLS

A Finalist for the 2015 Locus Award for Best Novella

The Citadel of Weeping Pearls was a great wonder; a perfect meld between cutting edge technology and esoteric sciences—its inhabitants capable of teleporting themselves anywhere, its weapons small and undetectable and deadly.

Thirty years ago, threatened by an invading fleet from the Dai Viet Empire, the Citadel disappeared and was never seen again.

But now the Dai Viet Empire itself is under siege, on the verge of a war against an enemy that turns their own mindships against them; and the Empress, who once gave the order to raze the Citadel, is in desperate needs of its weapons. Meanwhile, on a small isolated space station, an engineer obsessed with the past works on a machine that will send her thirty years back, to the height of the Citadel's power.

But the Citadel's disappearance still extends chains of grief and regrets all the way into the fraught atmosphere of the Imperial Court; and this casual summoning of the past might have world-shattering consequences...

THE OBSIDIAN AND BLOOD TRILOGY

Servant of the Underworld
Harbinger of the Storm
Master of the House of Darts

Year One-Knife, Tenochtitlan the capital of the Aztecs. Human sacrifice and the magic of the living blood are the only things keeping the sun in the sky and the earth fertile.

A Priestess disappears from an empty room drenched in blood. It should be a usual investigation for Acatl, High Priest of the Dead--except that his estranged brother is involved, and the the more he digs, the deeper he is drawn into the political and magical intrigues of noblemen, soldiers, and priests-and of the gods themselves...

"Amid the mud and maize of the Mexica empire, Aliette de Bodard has composed a riveting story of murder, magic, and sibling rivalry."
— *Elizabeth Bear, author of* All the Windwracked Stars

FOR NEWS ABOUT
JABBERWOCKY
BOOKS AND AUTHORS

Sign up for our newsletter*: http://eepurl.com/b84tDz
visit our website: awfulagent.com/ebooks
or follow us on twitter: @awfulagent

THANKS FOR READING!

*We will never sell or give away your email address, nor use
it for nefarious purposes. Newsletter sent out quarterly.

Made in the USA
Las Vegas, NV
29 November 2022